PRAISE FOR
Scared Stiff

"The clever sleuthing and intriguing setting will make readers want to ride this one to the finish."—*Publishers Weekly*

"The brisk pace, fluid style, and excitement of the novel are sure to entertain readers."
—*School Library Journal*

**DON'T MISS THESE OTHER
WILLO DAVIS ROBERTS MYSTERIES:**

Scared Stiff

WILLO DAVIS ROBERTS

ALADDIN

NEW YORK LONDON TORONTO SYDNEY NEW DELHI

ALADDIN

An imprint of Simon & Schuster Children's Publishing Division
1230 Avenue of the Americas, New York, New York 10020
This Aladdin paperback edition April 2016
Text copyright © 1991 by Willo Davis Roberts
Cover illustration copyright © 2016 by Jessica Handelman
Also available in an Aladdin hardcover edition.
All rights reserved, including the right of reproduction
in whole or in part in any form.
ALADDIN is a trademark of Simon & Schuster, Inc., and related logo
is a registered trademark of Simon & Schuster, Inc.
For information about special discounts for bulk purchases,
please contact Simon & Schuster Special Sales at 1-866-506-1949
or business@simonandschuster.com.
The Simon & Schuster Speakers Bureau can bring authors
to your live event. For more information or to book an event contact
the Simon & Schuster Speakers Bureau at 1-866-248-3049
or visit our website at www.simonspeakers.com.
Cover designed by Jessica Handelman
Interior designed by Mike Rosamilia
The text of this book was set in New Century Schoolbook.
Manufactured in the United States of America 1217 OFF
4 6 8 10 9 7 5 3
Library of Congress Control Number 2015958584
ISBN 978-1-4814-4911-3 (hc)
ISBN 978-1-4814-4910-6 (pbk)
ISBN 978-1-4814-4912-0 (eBook)

Scared Stiff

Chapter One

Troubles come in threes, Pa always said. I knew it was true. When my little brother Kenny broke his arm falling out of a tree, Pa said there'd be two more catastrophes before long, and sure enough, there were.

The very next day I cut my thumb on a tuna fish can and had to have three stitches, and a week later Ma lost a contact down the bathroom sink. We had insurance that took care of the emergency room charges on the first two, but we had to pay for the new contact, and it meant Pa couldn't buy the boots he'd been counting on.

So I guessed, when Pa came home and told us a load of new TVs he'd been hauling had been swiped while he was parked in a truck stop, that we were in for a whole lot of trouble.

I hoped the next two things wouldn't be as bad as the first one.

Pa was in a real bad mood when he told us. Ma licked her lips and asked, "Are they blaming you?"

His mouth was twisted and ugly. "Well, nobody's given me any medal for it. The truck and the load are my responsibility, as dispatch pointed out."

Ma pushed back a lock of dark hair with the back of her hand. She'd been stirring spaghetti sauce and was holding a wooden spoon, and she didn't even notice when the sauce dripped onto her blouse. "Are they going to fire you?"

Pa kicked the leg of a chair so it came out from the table and sat down, scowling. "It wasn't my fault, but when did that ever matter to E and F?"

E and F were Edward and Frank, partners in E & F Alberts Trucking. E was fat and always joking, and F was skinny and bald. Edward gave me gum when I went into the office with Pa sometimes, but I sort of liked Frank better. He remembered my first name and called me Rick instead of *Sonny*.

I stood in the doorway, waiting, because if Pa got fired it might mean we'd have to move, and I didn't want to move. And it might even mean Ma would lose her job, too, because she was the bookkeeper at E & F Alberts Trucking.

Ma noticed the spoon was dripping and put it back in the pot. I could tell she was upset. "So they haven't talked to you yet? You don't know if they'll fire you?"

Pa swore. "Who cares? A good driver can get a job anywhere," he said.

Kenny came up behind me, his eyes wide. He's only seven, and usually he's not paying much attention to what's going on with the rest of us, but nobody could listen to Pa's voice and not realize it was something serious this time. Once he was out of work for more than a month, and it made him pretty bad-tempered.

Kenny looked at me, but I shook my head. I didn't know how bad it was yet.

"Anywhere," Ma echoed. She didn't want to move any more than I did.

"Don't sweat it," Pa said, but now he sounded bleak rather than mad. "I'm not fired yet. I had to talk to the cops for over an hour. Maybe they'll get the stuff back."

A whole semi-load of TVs would be worth a lot of money. It made my mouth dry to think about it. I hoped they wouldn't expect Pa to pay for them. There was never quite enough money to go around anyway, without something like this going wrong.

Ma noticed us standing there. "Rick, you and Kenny go wash up. Supper's almost ready."

I wanted to hear what they were going to say, but in a way I didn't want to. I heard Ma ask, "What happened? Where were you when they got it? Did they take the trailer and all?"

"What do you *think*?" Pa said. "They took the stuff off box by box without getting caught?"

Ma looked hurt, the way she did when he was sarcastic.

"Yes, they took the entire trailer, while I was eating supper! I stopped at the place I always stop when I go that route. There was this guy who had to tarp up. I helped him do it before his load got wet, and he offered to buy me a steak."

"Was he anybody you knew?" Ma asked.

It seemed a simple question, and I didn't quite understand why it made Pa more irritated.

"No. I never saw him before. I don't even know his real name; he said they call him Bones. Because he's so skinny, I guess. I helped him with the tarp, and then we went inside to eat. My rig was parked out back, the way it usually is. I wasn't in the restaurant more than half an hour, and when I came out, my trailer was gone!"

Pa was so angry that I pushed Kenny ahead of me down the hall to the bathroom and shut the door behind us so we couldn't hear the rest.

Supper was good, but nobody ate much of it. Nobody talked, either. I'd got an *A* on a math paper, and ordinarily I'd have bragged about it, but not tonight. It hurt to swallow, and an *A* didn't seem to mean much.

I heard my folks talking after we'd gone to bed, though the only time I could make out the words was when they raised their voices. There was Ma's soft murmur, and then Pa practically thundered, "What kind of question is that to ask your husband? No, I didn't have anything to do with it!"

It took me a few minutes to figure out that she must have asked if he'd helped someone steal his trailer and load. Pa wouldn't do that, I thought, he couldn't steal. But she'd asked him, and now he was madder than ever.

Eleven's too old to cry, but it was hard not to. After that they went in their own bedroom and the murmur grew so low that I couldn't make out any of it.

It was a long time before I went to sleep, wondering what awful thing was going to happen next.

I found out first thing in the morning. While we were eating our oatmeal with brown sugar on it, Ma told us Pa was gone.

I put down my spoon, feeling all still and sickish inside. "Gone?" I repeated softly. "Gone where?"

"I don't know where," Ma said. Her voice was flat, and her hand trembled when she picked up her coffee cup. She tried to smile, but it didn't work very well. "It looks like it's going to be just you and me, boys."

I struggled with panic. "You don't mean Pa's *left*? For good?"

"I'm afraid so."

She looked at me then, and put down her cup to reach for my hand. "Rick, you know we haven't been getting along so well for a long time now."

I knew. I'd heard them arguing after they thought I was asleep.

"But he can't have gone!" I protested hollowly. "Not without even saying good-bye to Kenny and me!"

"I'm afraid he did, Rick."

I remembered all the things Pa and I were going to do together. Like the trips he'd promised me, one to Wyoming sometime when he had a load out there this summer, to where you could still see wild antelope grazing on the hills. Or maybe to Texas, to the Gulf of Mexico, where he'd seen dolphins playing in the surf off the beach.

Kenny was starting to cry. He went over to Ma and she hugged him.

I wanted to be hugged, too, but I just sat there. First Pa had his load and his trailer stolen, and now he was gone. My throat hurt when I swallowed. I reckoned there couldn't be anything much worse that could happen.

Or could there? I was almost sick to my stomach, wondering what the third big trouble would be.

I could never have guessed it would be as bad as it was.

For a few days I kept hoping that Pa would be there when I got home from school. He'd been mad enough to walk out and slam the door before, but up to now he'd always come home, late, not so mad anymore.

He didn't come, though. Once I walked into the living room in the evening when Ma was talking on the phone to her friend Sally Pope and I heard her say, "I hope he cares enough about the boys to send me part of his paycheck to take care of them. I can't swing the rent on this apartment all by myself for very long."

I backed out before Ma saw me. Kenny wanted to know what was the matter when I walked into our bedroom, and I shook my head. "I'm just missing Pa, I guess."

Kenny was building a spaceship with Legos on the floor between our beds. "I miss him, too. He was going to bring me a real turquoise belt buckle the next time he went to Albuquerque. Do you think he still will, Rick?"

"Sure, probably," I said, but it was more to make him feel better than because I believed it.

We were used to Pa being gone, because he drove an eighteen-wheeler all over the country and was only home between trips. Sometimes he didn't bring anything but an empty Thermos bottle and his dirty clothes. But we never knew when he might show up with a bag of kiwi fruits from California, or grapefruit from Arizona, or T-shirts from anywhere.

The neatest shirt he ever brought me made Ma roll her eyes. It was white, and there was a big black shark on the front and the words *Shark Attack!* The best part was the red splashes of "blood" all over, and the hole in one side with jagged teeth marks, like a shark had torn it out. When I wore it to school, Mr. Mellon suggested that now everyone had seen it, I should save it for weekends. The kids thought it was neat, except for Emmy Lou Wiggins. Emmy Lou said it was gross.

It wasn't just for the presents I wanted Pa

back, though. When he and Ma weren't arguing about something, we played Pictionary or went over to the park and played catch. Sometimes we'd go to the lake with a picnic lunch and swim.

It made my throat ache to think of never doing those things anymore, and I kept hoping Pa would at least send a postcard with palm trees or mountains or something on it.

Ma went to work every day, and Kenny and I went to school; there was no word from Pa until one day when I took the mail out of the box and there was an envelope that had his handwriting on it.

I couldn't wait for Ma to get home from work to give it to her. "It's thick," I pointed out. "Maybe he wrote a big long letter."

"Richard Van Huler, write a letter?" she asked, but I could see she was hoping he had.

There wasn't any letter, though. Just a stack of twenty-dollar bills. The paper folded around them was blank.

Ma sighed as she counted the money. "Well, at least I can pay the rent for this next month. Where was it mailed?"

I'd already looked at the postmark. "St. Louis. That's not so far away. Maybe he'll come home soon."

Ma looked at me sadly. "Honey, don't count on it," she said.

Chapter Two

It was hard not to hope Pa would come back. And the third big trouble hadn't happened yet. It made me nervous, because usually troubles in threes came close together.

And then it did happen.

Kenny and I were walking home from school. It was the last week, and I was carrying a bunch of stuff I'd cleaned out of my locker and my desk. Kenny didn't have as much, but he was loaded down, too.

We were late, because I'd stayed to play ball after school was out and Kenny had sat and watched. Ma didn't want him to go home alone, nor even cross streets by himself, because he was usually daydreaming and forgot to look both ways.

Anyway, as we turned the corner onto our

street, we saw Ma getting off the bus four blocks down. She waved, but we couldn't wave back because we had our arms full.

We kept walking toward each other, and we saw a car pull in alongside Ma.

"Who's that talking to Ma?" Kenny asked.

"Somebody asking for directions, probably," I said, shifting the heavy stuff because my arm was beginning to ache.

At first Ma didn't stop, though she turned her head when the driver of the car spoke to her. They were too far away, and the light reflected off the windshield, so I couldn't see what he looked like, or if there was more than one person in the car.

Ma kept walking, and the car drove very slowly beside her. I wished she'd hurry up, so she could help carry my stuff before my arms dropped off.

"I bet she's going to stop at Willie's," Kenny said. "She said she didn't have anything to cook for supper. Maybe she'll buy hot dogs," he added hopefully.

"She won't," I said positively. Pa was the only one who ever bought hot dogs. Ma said they were full of fat and not good for you. She was the only one who was kind of plump and needed to diet, but she was always worrying about what the rest of us ate.

The car kept coming, very slowly, along the curb on the side where no parking was allowed. Ma suddenly stopped and stood there, and the car stopped, too.

They were closer now, but there was still sun shining off the windshield and I didn't recognize the driver, though I thought it was a man.

When Kenny called to her, she turned toward us, and Kenny started to run.

"Ma! Can we have hot dogs tonight? Please?"

She glanced quickly at whoever was in the car, then took a few steps toward us, opening her purse. "All right. Here, get the hot dogs and the rest of what's on my list," she said, handing over the paper and several bills.

I stared at her in dismay. "We can't carry any groceries besides what we've already got," I protested.

"Then give me that stuff, and you get the

groceries," she said, and reached for my notebook and papers. "I'll meet you back home in a few minutes."

I felt uneasy right then, though I couldn't have said why. Maybe it was only because she'd so easily agreed to hot dogs, because that probably meant she wasn't thinking about what Kenny had asked for.

Still, there wasn't any reason not to do what she said. I handed over my stuff and headed for the side street where Willie's Grocery & Deli was. Kenny was going to stay with her, but Ma said sharply, "No, go on with Rick, honey."

So we went around the corner, leaving Ma there talking to the guy in the car. I looked back at the last minute and caught a glimpse of him: dark and bulky, the driver was, and wearing glasses with gold rims that glinted where the sun hit them when he leaned out the window.

"I told you she'd let us have hot dogs," Kenny said happily, skipping to keep up with me. "Let's get the kind that swell all up when you cook 'em, okay, Rick?"

We got the stuff on her list and paid Willie. When we came out of the side street, I looked for Ma, thinking we'd probably walk the rest of the way home together, across the street, but she was already gone.

"I'm going to have just ketchup on my hot dogs," Kenny said, as if I didn't know he didn't like mustard, the way the rest of us did. "I wish I'd asked if we could have potato chips, too."

"They're fried in grease," I reminded him. "She'd have said no."

There was more traffic now, in the street and on the sidewalk. A bunch of people got off another bus and were on the way home. I could smell frying potatoes and maybe pork chops. It smelled good, anyway, and I was glad hot dogs cooked fast.

Going up the steps to the apartment house, I paused. "Looks like Ma dropped my notebook," I said, frowning. "Somebody walked all over it and got it dirty. Can you pick it up, Kenny? It's the one with my frog sketches in it. I got an $A+$ on them."

Kenny retrieved the notebook, and I jiggled stuff around to get at my key, and we let ourselves into the little lobby. I squinted through the slit in the mailbox, but it was empty. Nothing from Pa. Of course, maybe Ma had already gotten it.

Usually our front door was locked and I had to use a key for that, too, but today it wasn't even quite closed. Well, Ma had expected us to be right behind her and had left it open for us, I thought. I called to her as soon as we were inside the apartment, but there was no answer. We walked through to the kitchen, and I put the grocery bag on the table and called again.

Nothing. A fly buzzed on the windowsill, but that was all. Upstairs I heard Mrs. Prather fixing supper; her walker thumped every time she moved.

"Where's Ma?" Kenny wanted to know.

She wasn't in the bathroom nor in her bedroom. She wasn't in the apartment at all, though she'd been there. The stuff she was carrying for me was there on the front-hall table, some of it spilling off onto the floor on top of the sweatshirt I'd dropped there yesterday. Ma was always after me to hang up something, I thought guiltily as I kicked it out of the way.

Maybe she'd gone across the hall to borrow something from Sally Pope. I went over there to see, but Sally shook her head. "Haven't seen her today," she said.

There wasn't anybody else in the building Ma would be visiting. She wouldn't even have gone to Sally's this close to suppertime unless she needed something she'd forgotten from the store.

So where was she, then?

I picked up the stuff that had fallen on the floor, added the notebook she'd dropped outside, and dumped it all on my bed.

"I'm hungry," Kenny said, almost whining.

"Yeah, me too," I agreed. "Let's go ahead and start fixing supper. Ma'll come back in a few minutes, I guess."

But she didn't.

We heated the hot dogs until they were fat and juicy, and I opened a can of corn and warmed up the buns. Ma would have made salad, but I wasn't very good at that and I figured one meal without it wouldn't hurt too much.

Kenny turned the burner off under the hot dogs and looked at me uncertainly.

"What do we do now? Where's Ma?"

"I don't know. I guess we better eat without her. She must have been delayed somewhere," I said.

So we ate, but my appetite wasn't as good as it had been earlier. I was getting worried, because Ma had never done this before.

When I thought of Billy Cowan, my stomach suddenly cramped. Billy wasn't in sixth grade, only in fifth, so I didn't know him too well, but everybody in school knew what had happened to him.

He'd been worried because his folks were fighting and he was afraid they were going to get a divorce, but he wasn't prepared for what they actually did. One day he came home and found everything gone out of the apartment except the stuff in his own room. His mother and dad had split, and each of them thought the other one would take Billy, but they didn't wait to see. They moved out, separately, and never bothered to check on Billy. They just abandoned him.

Mrs. Ratzloff, the school nurse, saw him crying on the front steps and stopped to find out what was the matter. Billy's in a foster home now, and he likes it okay, but he's always afraid his foster parents will get tired of him, too.

Pa wasn't tired of Kenny and me, I thought, but I guessed he was tired of Ma. Anyway, he left all three of us. What if Ma left, too?

She wouldn't, I thought, my chest aching so it was painful to breathe. Not ever.

But I jumped up from the table and went to her room and threw open the closet door, just in case.

All her dresses were still there. I jerked open a dresser drawer, and it was still full of underwear.

So we hadn't been abandoned.

But where was Ma?

We didn't clean up the food from the table, thinking surely Ma would be there any minute, starving, not minding that we hadn't made salad. She'd want to eat right away.

But she didn't come, and it got dark enough so we turned on the lights in the living room. Kenny turned on the TV, too, but I didn't pay any attention to what was on.

Finally it was time for Kenny to go to bed, and there was still no sign of Ma.

I didn't know what to do. I couldn't think of anybody to call. If Pa was here, he'd know what to do, I thought, and I began to be angry. It was his job to take care of us, so why wasn't he here?

I made Kenny take his bath and put on his pj's, and I read him a chapter from *Nothing's Fair in Fifth Grade* and then put him to bed.

He looked up at me gravely. "Rick, why isn't Ma here?"

"I don't know, but she'll come," I told him.

"Soon?"

I covered up the teddy bear he always slept with. "Soon," I promised, but I didn't believe it.

If something hadn't happened, she'd have been here a long time ago.

I went out and sat in the empty living room and waited, but nobody came.

Should I call the police? My heart pounded as I thought about it. Finally I got up and went to the telephone. You dialed 911, I knew, and they would send a police officer. If he didn't figure out right away where Ma was, would he take Kenny and me away, as an officer had done with Billy?

But we weren't abandoned, I told myself fiercely. Ma would never do that. Once, right after Pa left, I'd started to cry, just a little bit. And Ma hugged me and assured me we'd be all right, the three of us, even if Pa didn't come back.

"I don't see how he could do it," I said. "He always said he loved us!"

"He still loves you and Kenny," she told me softly, giving me a handkerchief to blow my nose. "It's only me he doesn't want to deal with anymore."

"But he used to love you too! Did *you* stop loving *him*? How can you stop loving someone?"

She hugged me again. "It happens sometimes, honey. Nobody wants it to happen, but sometimes it does. I don't know yet if I've stopped loving your pa or not. But Rick, I'm still here, and I'll always be here for you and Kenny. I promise."

Something happened to her, I thought. But what?

There was a pad beside the telephone, and

what Ma had written on it jumped out at me before I lifted the receiver.

Uncle Henry, Ma had written, and there was a number after his name. *Message, Mrs. Biggers.*

Uncle Henry, I thought. Yes, he was the one to call. He was about the only relative we had, except for my snooty Aunt Susan, who lives in Philadelphia. She's Ma's sister, but she married a rich lawyer that neither Ma or Pa could ever stand, and I only saw them twice. Both times they acted like we weren't good enough for them, Pa said.

Uncle Henry didn't have a telephone of his own. He lived in a remodeled school bus, Ma told us. Uncle Henry was old, and crotchety sometimes, but he was nicer than Aunt Susan, and he lived a lot closer, too, right in our same town in Indiana.

My fingers were shaking as I dialed the number on the pad.

Mrs. Biggers was brusque when she told me Uncle Henry wasn't there. "He works as a night watchman, you know."

"Oh." I must have sounded as forlorn as I felt.

"You want me to give him a message?" she asked.

I swallowed and hesitated. Should I wait until morning to reach Uncle Henry, or should I call the police tonight?

"Is it important?" she asked. And then, sounding more kind, "An emergency?"

I gulped. "Yes. It's an emergency. Tell him . . . tell him Rick called. My mom . . . my mom's disappeared. I think . . . I think something bad has happened to her," I said.

Chapter Three

It wasn't like on TV, where a whole bunch of cops come with their lights flashing and the sirens going.

Only one officer came up the stairs. He had a notebook and he asked questions and wrote down the answers, but he didn't seem to think anything really bad had happened to Ma.

"She may just be visiting a friend," he suggested.

I swallowed so hard it hurt. "Her only friend in the building is Sally, across the hall. She hasn't been there."

"A friend outside the building," the cop said. He sounded bored, as if this kind of thing happened all the time and it was never important.

The door behind him was pushed further

open, and Uncle Henry stuck his head in. "What's going on?" he wanted to know.

Uncle Henry is pretty old. He has thin white hair and faded blue eyes, and a lot of wrinkles in his face. I guessed Mrs. Biggers had managed to get hold of him somehow, and I felt better immediately. He'd know what to do.

I told the story again, and once more the cop said, "She's probably visiting a friend." He looked at me and added, "Outside the building. Maybe she went with this guy you saw her talking to, in the car."

"She didn't," I said desperately. "She came home. We know that, because she brought my school stuff and put it on the table. And it was suppertime. She always cooks supper. And the only time she ever leaves us alone in the apartment is right after school. And not for more than an hour."

"Who was the man in the car?" Uncle Henry wanted to know.

"I don't know. I never saw him before. And . . ." I hesitated, because I was only guessing, and then I blurted, "I don't think she liked him, whoever he was. I could tell by her face. He was sort of making her talk to him, driving along beside her so slow, but she would never have gone anywhere with him. Besides, she came home. She brought my stuff."

The officer closed his notebook and put his pen back in his pocket. "You, sir, you're the boys' uncle?"

"Great-uncle," Uncle Henry corrected him. "You're going to look for my niece, aren't you? Rick is right. This isn't like Sophie. She wouldn't go off and leave her kids alone."

"Well, if she doesn't show up in the morning, I'd suggest you come down to headquarters and file a missing-persons report. She probably went off on her own, and she'll come back when she's ready."

My eyes stung. It wasn't true. Ma would never have gone off and left us.

And then I remembered. Pa had.

I sounded fierce. "She didn't! She's hurt or something! She didn't go anywhere unless someone made her!"

The officer gave me a cool look, then spoke to Uncle Henry. "This kind of thing happens all the time, sir, and almost always the person shows up safe and sound, on their own."

"Not Sophie Van Huler," Uncle Henry asserted. "You'll see. If she could come home, she'd be here now."

"You check in with us in the morning, sir." The cop looked at me. "You going to see to the children, Mr. Svoboda? I mean, I can't leave them here in an empty apartment."

I looked at Uncle Henry in panic. Would they put Kenny and me into a foster home or something? Like Billy?

"Yes, yes, certainly, I'll see to the boys," Uncle Henry said impatiently, waving a hand.

"You give us a call in the morning. Let us know when Mrs. Van Huler comes home," the officer said.

"*If* she comes home," Uncle Henry said.

It was only after the officer had gone that Uncle Henry noticed my face.

"Of course she'll come back, Rick. It's only that the police, with their wait-and-see attitude, make me angry. No doubt many of the people they are called upon to find *do* walk off of their own accord. If they knew Sophie, they'd know *she* wouldn't do that. Where's your father? Off on a trip, is he?"

So Ma hadn't told him. I had to.

Uncle Henry was sober. "Good thing the officer didn't know that, or he'd think your ma was so upset about your pa that she forgot about you two, and we know that's not the case. Well, look here, I've got to get back to work. I'm a night watchman, you know, and I only got your message because I forgot my arthritis medicine and had to come home for it on my supper break, and Mrs. Biggers saw me. I've got to get back. You throw a few things in a suitcase—you got a suitcase?—or a paper bag, clothes and your toothbrushes, that kind of thing, and we'll get your brother and go."

I was still worried about Ma, but at least the police weren't going to take us to a foster home, and Uncle Henry would see to us.

"Shall I get Kenny dressed? Or leave him in his pajamas?"

"Bring him the way he is. I got my house right out in the street; we'll put him to bed right away."

Startled, I paused before I went after the clothes we'd need. "Your house is in the street?"

"Live in a school bus. Thought your ma'd have told you that, when she talked to me last week. I called to tell her where I was. Good thing, considering this. Mind, I'm not set up to take care of a couple of kids indefinitely, but your ma'll show up shortly, no doubt. We'll manage until she does."

The school bus was sort of startling when we got there. I'd expected a yellow bus, like the ones some of the kids rode to school, but this one was painted purple. With bright-colored swirls and flowers all over it.

Uncle Henry saw me looking at it as we crossed the street, and snorted. "Fancy, isn't it? Never would have painted it that way myself, but that's the way it was when the feller handed it over to me."

Kenny staggered between us, still half asleep. Uncle Henry opened the door of the purple bus, and I boosted Kenny up the steps and stopped, astonished.

On the outside it looked weird, but inside it was wonderful.

"It's like a real house!" I said, pushing Kenny toward the couch on one side. Opposite the couch was a table with two benches upholstered just like the couch in striped brown and tan fabric. There was a television and a tiny kitchen, and through a door beyond that I could see a bed.

"I only got the one bed," Uncle Henry said, coming in behind us. "I work nights and sleep days, so I'll have to keep on sleeping back there. You kids'll have to sleep on the couch. It opens up. Here, Kenny, stand up, and I'll show you."

"I never saw a TV in a bus before," Kenny said sleepily.

"No TV tonight, and none played loud when I'm sleeping," Uncle Henry said, opening up our bed. "I'm a bit hard of hearing, but not deaf, you know. My only other sheets are in the washing—I get Mrs. Biggers to do my laundry—but I have a blanket for you. You need to use the bathroom before you crawl into bed?"

"You have a bathroom in your bus, too?" Kenny asked, impressed.

"How else am I going to live in it?" Uncle Henry asked. "I'm too old to be going out to a public restroom. Door on the right, just before the bedroom."

It was tiny, but it had a toilet and a wash basin and a shower. If I hadn't been so upset about Ma, I'd have enjoyed seeing it all.

When I went back out front, Uncle Henry was starting the engine. I slid into the other seat, hoping he wouldn't make me go to bed right away.

"It's so nice inside," I said. "So different from what it looks like on the outside." Then I was afraid I'd insulted him, and I didn't know what to say next.

Uncle made that snorting sound again, and I decided it was the way he laughed. "That's the whole point," he said. "Places I have to park it sometimes, I don't want anybody to think it's any more than a hippy bus, full of junk. Don't want 'em ripping off my TV and stereo and such. To look at it from the outside, nobody'd bother with it. I keep the curtains closed, so they can't see in."

We were moving through the darkened

streets now. "You just live in this? And you park it on the street?"

"No, no. Not very often, anyway. Stay at the Wonderland RV Park." He made that snorting sound again.

"That sounds . . . interesting," I observed.

"Sounds more interesting than it is," Uncle Henry said.

He didn't talk anymore, and I couldn't think of anything else to say, either. I wanted to be reassured that everything would be all right, that Ma would indeed show up safe and sound in the morning, that Pa would come back.

Uncle Henry wasn't too used to kids, I guess; he only saw us when he came over for dinner for his birthday, or Ma's, or on Christmas Eve when we opened presents together. But last year he gave me a Swiss army knife, and it was a neat one with all kinds of blades and tools, so I knew he was kind. Ma must have told him what I wanted, and he'd brought it, and even wrapped it in pretty paper.

If he thought everything would be all right, he'd probably have said so.

He didn't, though, and it made me afraid to ask what he thought.

I didn't know what we'd do if Ma didn't come home.

On the ride through the mostly darkened city I thought it all through in my mind again, how that guy in the car had been driving slowly beside Ma, and how when we got up to her she'd sent us to Willie's for the groceries— almost as if she wanted us away from her while she talked to the man in the car—and how my school stuff was in the apartment so we knew she'd been there, except for the notebook she'd dropped on the steps.

What had happened to her?

Had she sent us to Willie's because she was afraid of the stranger? Did she know him? What if he'd followed her into the apartment house, and made her go away with him?

Why would he do that? And if he had, what did he mean to do to her? How could we convince the police to look for her? What if they couldn't find her, even if they did look?

By the time we pulled in at the Wonderland RV Park, I was convinced Ma had been kidnapped. It was the last of the three troubles in this batch, and the worst of all. It was the worst trouble I'd ever been in in my whole life, and I didn't know what to do about it.

Chapter Four

Uncle Henry was right about the Wonderland RV Park. I don't know what I expected, exactly, but not rows of old trailers and a few motor homes, most of them pretty run down.

There weren't any more like the purple bus.

Uncle Henry had his own space, way at the back where, he said, the purple bus wouldn't scare off any overnighters. Overnighters were people who were traveling and only stopped there to sleep before going on.

They didn't have many tourists, though. Not since the Wonderland Amusement Park had been closed down over a year ago.

"That's why this place looks sort of tacky," Uncle Henry told us the next morning. "Mrs. Biggers—she's the manager, working for the heirs of the estate, the family that's fighting about what to do with the amusement park—does the best she can, but the Mixons don't want to spend any money, so she doesn't have anything to work with."

"Who are the Mixons?" Kenny asked. I could tell by his eyes that he'd cried himself to sleep.

"Family owns both the parks. Old Mr. Mixon built Wonderland and ran it for years, but when he died the heirs couldn't decide what to do with it. One granddaughter wanted to keep on running it, but the rest of them wanted to sell the property and divide up the money, so they're still battling it out. It's valuable industrial property, and they could get a lot of cash out of it. In the meantime, until it's settled, it's a cheap place for me to live, and close to the warehouse where I work," Uncle Henry said. "I walk to work."

I could see why it was cheap. Nothing had been painted or fixed in a while, it looked like. It didn't matter to me. I didn't intend to be there very long. Ma would surely be back soon, I thought.

Only she wasn't. Uncle Henry took us with

him when he went down to the police station and filed a missing-persons report. I thought they should call in the FBI, because I was certain Ma had been kidnapped—otherwise she'd have come home by now—but they said there was no evidence of kidnapping. She'd just run off for reasons of her own, the officer said.

It made my throat hurt to think about it. It couldn't be true; Ma wouldn't have abandoned us. I guess Uncle Henry knew how I felt, because he put his hand on my shoulder and squeezed it.

"Maybe we ought to go by the apartment on the way back to my place," he said as we left the station, "and see if you can find any of that evidence they think they have to have."

There wasn't any, though.

It felt awful, walking through the empty apartment. Ma's stuff was still there, same as we'd left it.

"What would be a clue?" Kenny asked. "Bloodstains?"

"Blood would mean somebody hurt her!" I said, getting sicker by the moment. I stared at Uncle Henry, who was looking through the stuff on Ma's desk. "We don't have any reason to think that, do we?"

"Not at all," Uncle Henry agreed. "Well, blamed if I can see anything that would make the police or the FBI go looking for her any sooner."

I could tell by his voice that he didn't expect them to do much, and I waited for Uncle Henry to take charge himself.

Instead, he sighed and put the things back on the desk. "Well, I guess there's nothing to do but wait for Sophie to show up. I'll check with the hospitals, make sure she didn't get hurt and have amnesia, something like that. The police are used to dealing with this kind of thing. Maybe they're right. Maybe your ma will show up on her own. No reason for anybody to kidnap her that I can think of, and not likely in broad daylight. They couldn't expect any rich relatives to pay a ransom, because she doesn't have any rich relatives."

Was he giving up, just like that? He couldn't, I thought. He just couldn't! What if he did, and we never got Ma back?

"What are we going to do, then?" I asked.

Uncle Henry looked around. "I guess you boys better pack some more clothes and bring them on back to my place. While you're doing that I'll check with the manager and see how long the rent's paid for."

He was back before we'd put our stuff into the old suitcases. "Got two weeks left," he announced. "Looks like there's enough money in her bank account to pay it for another month, but we can't get it without her signature, and I can't afford to pay it. Let's think positive. She'll likely turn up by then."

My eyes were kind of blurry. "This is the last day of school," I said, "and we've already missed the morning. There's supposed to be a party this afternoon."

"You want to go to the party?" Uncle Henry asked, and I shook my head.

"No." Up until Ma disappeared, it had sounded like fun, but no more. "I guess we've got to pick up our report cards, though."

"I'll call the school and explain the circumstances," Uncle Henry said, sounding gruff. "I should think they could mail them."

So we went back to the Wonderland RV

Park. "I need to sleep a few more hours before I go to work again," Uncle Henry said when we reentered the purple bus. "You kids help yourself to what you want to eat. I'll get some more stuff later, but there's plenty of peanut butter and jelly. You need anything, that's the manager's trailer over there, with the sign. Mrs. Biggers."

He disappeared into the back bedroom, and Kenny and I looked at each other.

"Isn't anybody going to find Ma?" he asked.

It didn't look like it, I thought. Not very fast, anyway, and what was happening to her in the meantime?

When I didn't answer him, Kenny said, "Pa would find her, if he knew she was missing. Wouldn't he, Rick?"

Would he? He and Ma had had a fight before he left, but I couldn't believe he'd let anybody get away with kidnapping her.

And he was one person who wouldn't believe she'd walked away on her own, just abandoning us.

Pa had.

The thought hurt as bad as when I'd

accidentally pounded a nail through my hand the time I was trying to build a birdhouse.

But when Pa left, he knew we still had Ma. Mothers usually got to have the kids when parents split up, didn't they? And Pa couldn't have taken us on the truck with him. Not for more than a single trip.

"Couldn't we call Pa?" Kenny asked hopefully.

"Where are we going to call him?" I asked, and hoped I didn't sound as if I was going to cry, even if I felt like I might. "We don't know where he is."

"Doesn't he still work for E & F?" Kenny asked.

I stared at him. "I don't know. Ma never said." Excitement began to grow inside me. "We can call E & F and find out if they can contact him."

"Uncle Henry doesn't have a phone," Kenny pointed out. From the bedroom Uncle Henry began to snore.

"Maybe there's a pay phone." I grimaced. "Well, we don't have any money. Let's get something to eat, and then we'll ask Uncle Henry when he gets up about calling."

After we'd eaten two peanut butter and jelly sandwiches apiece, though, and Uncle Henry was still asleep, we decided to go outdoors. There wasn't much to do inside except watch TV, and we were afraid it would be too loud. Besides, there was nothing on but soap operas.

In the afternoon sunshine, the Wonderland RV Park looked empty and boring. In a tiny trailer across from the purple bus an old lady was watering some red flowers in a box on her tiny deck, but there was nobody else around.

Kenny blinked against the sun and looked around. "There's no place to play," he pointed out. "No swings or merry-go-rounds or anything like that."

"It's right next to an amusement park," I said. "I suppose they expected the kids to go there and pay for rides."

We looked at the high gray wooden wall, and I tried to imagine what it was like on the other side. We'd been to an amusement park once when Ma and Kenny and I all went with Pa on a run to Fort Worth. The park was called Six Flags Over Texas, and I guess it was one of the most exciting places I'd ever been.

Kenny was only three then, and he didn't remember as much as I did, but he'd liked getting to drive an old-fashioned car. It was on a track, so it didn't really matter how he steered. We had a lot of fun, except Kenny ate too many hot dogs and threw up in the sleeper of the truck afterward. Pa swore and said he'd never take us to an amusement park again, at least not if we had to ride in his truck later.

Kenny kicked at a rock in the gravel drive. "I wish we could go in there, to the other park. Do you think it has a merry-go-round?"

"Probably," I said, remembering the one at Six Flags. *That* one was in a sort of open-sided house all by itself. It was beautiful and big, and the music made your blood feel sort of bubbly and happy, just to listen to it. "But it's locked up now and there are Keep Out signs. I saw them on the front gate when we came back here this time."

"I know a way in."

The voice startled me, and I spun around fast. I hadn't known there was anyone around.

The girl was about ten, I guessed. She had short dark hair, cut almost like a boy's, and she wore old jeans and a pink T-shirt that said *"Meaner than a junkyard dog"* under a picture of a snarling Doberman. She was wearing tiny little gold earrings.

I felt awkward around a strange girl, but intrigued by what she'd said. "You mean you know how to get into the Wonderland Amusement Park?"

She had bare brown feet in scruffy tennis shoes. "Are you the kids that are going to live with Mr. Svoboda?"

"We're not going to live with Uncle Henry," I denied quickly. "Only stay with him until Ma comes home."

"Oh. Grandma said your mother had disappeared. Mr. Svoboda told her so."

"Well, she did, but she's going to come back." I wanted desperately to believe that. "Who are you? Do you live here?"

She nodded. "I'm Julie Biggers. My grandma's the manager."

"Is there a telephone here?"

She gestured with a tanned thumb. "Pay phone in the laundry room."

"I don't have any money."

She tipped her head slightly to one side, considering. "I was hoping one of you would be a girl. There's nobody to play with around here. Well." She sounded resigned. "I suppose you could use the office phone. Grandma has to pay for it, though, so you can't make a long-distance call."

"It's to a trucking company where our pa works," I said. "It's right here in town."

"Come on, then," said Julie Biggers, and led the way to the manager's trailer.

It didn't look like much on the outside, but inside it wasn't bad except for being shabby. It was neat and clean.

Mrs. Biggers said okay when Julie asked if we could use the telephone. She was younger than Uncle Henry, but old enough to have a lot of lines in her face. "Phone's in the kitchen," she said. Something was cooking on the stove, sending out good-smelling steam. "You know the number you want?"

I shook my head, and she got out a telephone book for me to look it up. I found it all right, E & F Trucking, on Telegraph Avenue. I kept a finger on the number so I could dial it, and then decided to try our apartment first, just in case.

It rang and rang, and I could see the empty rooms in my imagination. Ma hadn't come back yet.

I swallowed the lump in my throat and dialed the number in the phone book.

The voice that answered was businesslike. "E & F Trucking. Cranston speaking."

Cranston was the dispatcher. He had never paid any attention to me the times I was in the office with Pa. Pa said he didn't like kids. Sometimes I thought he didn't like anybody. I heard him and Pa yelling at each other once, when Cranston said Pa had to deliver a load in Los Angeles by a certain time. Pa said, "Me and what airplane? No way I can drive that far that fast, not and stay even on the fringe of being legal." It had made me nervous to hear them sounding so angry with each other, and I'd gone outside and not listened to any more.

I was nervous now, too, enough so my voice squeaked a little. "This . . . this is Rick Van Huler," I said. "My pa is Van—Van Van Huler. I mean, that's his nickname. I need . . . I need to find out where he is, because something's happened to Ma—"

"Sophie? She didn't show up for work this morning," Cranston said crossly.

"Yes, sir, I know. She . . . we don't know where she is, and we need to talk to Pa. . . ."

"The office is a mess without her," Cranston said, sounding as if he thought it was my fault she wasn't there. "Merv's off on vacation, and Sophie doesn't show up, and there's a payroll to figure. Who's going to do that?"

He scared me, but I was too scared at the idea of not reaching Pa to give up. "Please, can you get in touch with my pa? Can you tell him Kenny and I are at Uncle Henry's, and we don't know where Ma is?"

"Look, kid, I'm busy. You see your ma, you tell her she's going to lose her job if she stays off without letting us know what's going on, okay? We need her to figure the payroll and get out the checks."

"But Pa," I said desperately, "we need him!"

"Van's on a run to Miami, Oklahoma," Cranston said. "Then he picks up a load for Ogallala. Due back here next Thursday. If I can remember it, I'll tell him you called."

I heard another phone ringing in the background, and he hung up on me.

I swallowed hard. If he could remember? What if he didn't remember?

Julie Biggers reached for an apple in a bowl on the table, watching me. "You want one?"

I shook my head. "No, thanks." The thought of eating anything made me queasy. Kenny took one, though.

"Did you get Pa?" he asked.

So I told him what the dispatcher had said. Mrs. Biggers was working at the counter, shaping loaves of bread. She brushed oil over the tops of the loaves and put them in the oven.

My voice wavered as I concluded, "So I don't know if he'll even tell Pa when he comes back."

"Write your father a letter, then," Mrs. Biggers suggested. "Julie, get him some paper and a pen and an envelope. Send it to the place where he works, and they'll surely see he gets it. It's a federal offense to interfere with anyone else's mail."

Julie went to get the materials for me to write a letter, and I stood there in the good-smelling kitchen, not knowing what else to do except to follow Mrs. Bigger's suggestion.

But this was Friday, and Thursday was a whole week away. What was happening to Ma? What if somebody kidnapped her not for ransom but to hurt her? What if she couldn't wait a whole week to be rescued?

The police weren't going to do anything except wait and see. Uncle Henry didn't seem to know anything to do, either. I was sure Pa would think of something, but he wouldn't know for at least a week.

What could I do in the meantime? Me, Rick Van Huler, one eleven-year-old kid?

I had to think of something to do, I had to help Ma. Only I couldn't think of anything at all.

Chapter Five

I thought hard about what to say in the letter and finally wrote in my best handwriting, "Dear Pa: We need you. Ma has disappeared, maybe been kidnapped. Kenny and I are staying with Uncle Henry in a purple school bus at the Wonderland RV Park. Please come home. Love, Rick."

I chewed on the pen for a minute before adding, "We miss you a lot."

I didn't say anything about how scared we were. I figured Pa was smart enough to figure that out for himself, and it sounded better this way.

Mrs. Biggers gave me a stamp and said Uncle Henry could pay for it later. "Julie can show you where to mail it," she told me.

It didn't seem like very much action to

take, but I couldn't think of anything else.

"There's a big mailbox out by the street," Julie said, and the three of us, she and Kenny and I, all went outside and walked toward the front of the Wonderland RV Park.

The old lady who watered her flowers peeked out the window at us and waved. Julie waved back.

"Mrs. Kenck," Julie said. "Her grandson is coming to visit in July for two weeks. He's a pretty good ball player. His name is Lael. If you're still here, maybe we can play work-up or something."

"We won't still be here," I said quickly.

"We'll go home before July, won't we, Rick?" Kenny asked, and I nodded hard.

"Once Pa gets this letter, he'll come and get us," I said. I didn't add, "whether Ma comes back before then or not," because I didn't even want to think about Ma not coming back.

The big mailbox was apparently for everybody who lived in the RV park. There weren't any houses along this street, only a lot of warehouses and the Wonderland Amusement Park, which was surrounded by a high wooden wall, painted gray, that we couldn't see over.

As if she read my thoughts, Julie said, "It's not a very good neighborhood to live in. No kids. I have to take a bus to school. This was the last day; we came home right after noon. If you have to go to school from here, I'll show you where to catch the bus."

I was almost angry with her. "We won't be here long enough to go back to school."

She didn't seem offended. "Your mom and dad both went away and left you, huh?"

I put my letter in the box and shoved up the red metal flag so the mailman would take the letter. "Our pa's a long-haul truck driver, and he's gone to Oklahoma for a week. And Ma didn't go away and leave us. Something happened to her."

"Something bad?" Julie asked quietly.

My eyes burned. "We don't know for sure, but she'd never have gone away and left us on purpose."

Kenny had found a dead bird and squatted down to look at it more closely. He looked up now and asked, "Did your mom and dad go away and leave you? Is that why you live with your grandma?"

"My dad has a job in Alaska," Julie said, nudging the dead bird with the toe of one red tennis shoe. "He's not home very much, and he said it's no place for a kid, so he sent me here. Living with Grandma's not so bad. I miss my mom, though."

"Where's she?" Kenny demanded.

"In California. She works for a senator, and she travels a lot. She couldn't make a living for the two of us here, she said. She has to go where the money is. Besides, she just has a little apartment; she isn't there very much, and she couldn't leave me alone, either, any more than Daddy could. So it's better I'm here."

She didn't really sound as if she thought so. But at least she knew where her parents were. She changed the subject.

"Do you want to see inside of Wonderland?"

Kenny stood up. We were on the sidewalk, and from here we could see what I'd only glimpsed last night. The wall around the amusement park was blank on the side next to the RV park, but at the front there was a big solid gate we couldn't see through and a fancy sign covered with colored light bulbs. A lot of them were broken.

"I never saw it lighted up," Julie said, looking up at it, too. "Grandma says Wonderland was one of the biggest and best amusement parks in Indiana when she first came here. But that was many years ago, before I was born."

"There's a Keep Out, No Trespassing sign," I observed. "It looks like it's been closed for quite a while."

"Ever since Mr. Mixon died," Julie agreed. "Grandma thinks eventually the family will agree to sell it to the company that has the warehouses beyond it; they want more room and they've offered to buy it. Then they'd get rid of the stuff inside, and tear down the wall to make another warehouse."

The gray wall went down the whole block, so it was big, all right. Bigger than several of the huge warehouses across the street and on the other side of the park.

"We don't know what will happen to us if they sell," Julie said, looking up at the sign with the broken lights. "Grandma says we couldn't afford rental space for her trailer anywhere else, if she wasn't the manager. Of course Daddy sends her money to take care of me, but I guess it costs a lot to buy my clothes and feed me. Did you ever go to a big amusement park?"

"Once," I said. "Six Flags Over Texas. It was neat." I remembered, then, what she'd said a while ago. "Did you say you've been inside this one? What's it like?"

Julie looked quickly around, as if to make sure she wasn't overheard. Two elderly men were talking in front of the nearest trailer, but they weren't close enough to hear what we said.

"Nobody's supposed to go in there. You'd have to promise not to tell."

Kenny's eyes were bright with interest. "It's locked. Do you have the keys?"

"No. But there's a secret way in."

"Did you break in?" I was still interested, too, but a little uncomfortable about breaking the law. I knew what Ma would think about that, even if the park was sort of abandoned.

"I didn't have to," Julie said. "But I found

out there was a way in. So I go there sometimes. It's the only thing there is to do around
here that's worthwhile, except reading. And
the library's so far away I can't get there more
than once a week, on the bus. We can't go into
Wonderland right now, though. There are too
many people around."

The only people I could see were the two old
men and the woman who had just come out to
sweep her little scrap of sidewalk in front of a
tiny trailer not much bigger than a car.

"What's in there?" Kenny asked, staring at
the blank gray boards as if he had X-ray eyes.
"Can we ride a merry-go-round? Or the Ferris
wheel? Is there a roller coaster?"

"There's all of them," Julie said, "only you
can't ride any of them. They're shut down."
She saw his disappointment and added quickly,
"But there's a lot of stuff to look at and play on.
I sit in the moon rocket and pretend I'm head-
ing out into space. It's neat."

If I hadn't been so worried about Ma, I'd
have been more excited. Still, I didn't see what
I could do except wait to hear from Pa. All my
life I'd been told that if you get in trouble, you

call the cops. Now we had, and they weren't going to do anything. Uncle Henry said it was because they were used to dealing with irresponsible people, and there were plenty of them who *did* walk off and leave their families; the police dealt with so many like that, they assumed everyone was that way. They didn't know Ma, or they'd be looking for her right this minute.

I figured I might as well find something else to think about, if I could, and Wonderland was as good as anything. "When do we go in, then?" I asked.

Julie grinned and spoke in a conspiratorial whisper, looking down the road between the rows of trailers. "Well, if we're lucky, Mrs. Bogen will go off shopping pretty soon. If she does, we can go right away, because she's the only one who could see us, and she'd tell Grandma for sure. If she doesn't shop today, though, we'll have to wait until tonight," she said. "As soon as it's dark."

"In the dark?" Kenny asked, dismayed. "We have to go in the dark?" Kenny likes to sleep with a night-light on.

"If we don't want to get caught we have to go when nobody will notice us. Everybody who lives here is retired, and all they have to do is sit around and watch what everybody else is doing," Julie explained. "They notice who visits who, and when they go away, and things like that."

I could tell by his face that Kenny hoped we wouldn't wait until dark.

"Where do we go in?" he asked. "There's no doors or windows, and the big gate is fastened shut."

Julie looked mysterious. "It's a secret way I found. I'll show you. As soon as it's dark. Or if Mrs. Bogen leaves to shop. She drives that little blue car, and it always takes her three or four hours because she stops to visit her sister on the way home. If you see her car leave, meet me as soon as you can over by the laundry room."

So we had to wait to visit Wonderland, too. It wasn't as bad as waiting for Ma to come back, or Pa to show up; but as the day went on I could see Kenny was almost as nervous as he was looking forward to an adventure, and I sort of felt that way myself. When he said he hoped we wouldn't have to wait until after dark, I had to agree.

It was hot in the sun, and there were only a few spindly little shade trees, none of them near the purple bus, so we went inside.

Kenny was hungry, and I looked to see what there was to eat. Uncle Henry sure had different ideas from Ma about food, I decided. There was nothing to make a salad, which was okay; I wouldn't have made one anyway, but it seemed strange to find the vegetable bin full of kielbasa sausage and baloney and Mars bars. The bread wasn't brown, like the kind we had at home, but when I made sandwiches out of the baloney and white bread, they weren't too bad. There were a lot of Mars bars, so I hoped it was okay if we each had one of those, too. Ma almost never bought candy.

Everything reminded me of Ma. Whether it was the same as she did things, or totally different, it all made me feel like crying.

What if Ma never came back again? We couldn't stay here in this old school bus with Uncle Henry, sleeping on a couch in his living room. We couldn't go with Pa on the truck, with no sleeper space for three of us and having to eat in restaurants and nowhere to go to school or get our clothes washed. Would we have to be in a foster home, then? Or worse yet, go to live with Aunt Susan in Philadelphia?

Most of my worry wasn't for Kenny and me, though, but for Ma. I knew something bad had happened to her, no matter what the police thought. The more I considered the matter, the more convinced I was that she'd been afraid of the man in the car, that she'd deliberately sent Kenny and me away because of that. If one of us boys had been kidnapped, she'd be tearing the city apart trying to find us. She'd be yelling at the cops until they did something. We ought to be doing the same thing; but how could we, if they wouldn't listen to us?

Kenny was bored, and there was nothing to read that we could find except a stack of newspapers. We'd already read the comics in them, so I finally turned on the TV real low, so it wouldn't wake Uncle Henry. Several times I looked out the window, but Mrs. Bogen's little blue car was still sitting there.

Everything that was on TV seemed stupid. The characters were all grown-ups, and they were very serious and talked about a lot of other people who weren't there, and they hugged and kissed a lot. I don't know what Kenny was getting out of it.

Uncle Henry finally woke up and came out scratching his bare chest. "Time to think about supper," he said.

Ma wouldn't have let us eat that way for very long, but it was good. We had chili out of a can, with cheese melted on top of it, and chopped onions and nacho chips. For dessert there was chocolate-ripple ice cream with chocolate sauce.

"Tomorrow I'll get some vegetables," Uncle Henry said gruffly.

"That's all right," Kenny said politely. "We don't mind if there aren't any vegetables."

Uncle Henry grunted. I don't think he usually ate vegetables, but he knew kids were supposed to have them.

Finally he went and got his blue uniform shirt with the Security Patrol patch on the sleeve and the pocket. He had a gun, too, in a holster. He saw Kenny looking at it, bug-eyed.

"Don't you ever touch this, young'un," Uncle Henry said sternly. "I don't leave it lying around, but no matter where it is, don't you kids touch it."

"Is it loaded?" Kenny asked in awe.

"Of course it's loaded. What good would it be to me if I caught somebody trying to break into one of my buildings and my gun wasn't loaded? This is what's most important, though, right here."

He patted the cordless telephone he was attaching to his belt. "Call the cops if I need any help. Had to call them once, couple of months ago, when I caught two punks inside the warehouse. I didn't even let on I saw them until they started to carry out boxes to put in their pickup; I called 911 and just waited until those fellers were ready to leave. Then I stepped out and told them to freeze and held them there until the police showed up. Sent both of them to jail," he concluded with satisfaction.

He picked up his uniform cap. "Well, I have

to get going. I work a twelve-hour shift, except for Sundays and Mondays when Oliver takes over. I won't be back till about the time you boys will be getting up, I reckon. Nothing to worry about here, Mrs. Biggers keeps a good eye on everything." He snorted. "Far as that goes, so does everybody else. Most of them have nothing to do but look out their windows. I'll see you in the morning."

When he was gone, Kenny knelt on the couch to look out the window. "How will we know when it's dark enough to meet Julie?"

"It won't be dark for a couple of hours," I told him. In the next trailer over I saw a man and a woman eating their supper. They looked up and waved, smiling.

I waved back. It seemed strange to be so close to your neighbors that you could tell they were eating pork chops and baked potatoes and spinach.

And then, right while I was looking out the window, a lady in a yellow pantsuit came out of her trailer and got into the small blue car and drove away.

By the time I had relayed that to Kenny, I

saw Julie come out of Mrs. Biggers's trailer carrying a cardboard box and head for the laundry room.

"It's time," I said to Kenny. "It's time to explore Wonderland. Come on, let's go."

Chapter Six

Julie had unloaded little packages of bleach and detergent from the box she carried and put them into a dispenser. There was a fat lady in a flowered dress waiting for her to finish so she could put coins in the machine, and Julie put a warning finger on her lips behind the woman's back.

"Are we going to—" Kenny began, and I clapped a hand over his mouth just in time.

"We can go out this way, and I'll get rid of this box," Julie said when she'd finished, leading the way toward the back of the building.

Several washing machines were running noisily, and two driers were spinning clothes around. We walked between them and out into the sunshine before I dared take my hand off Kenny's mouth.

"What'd you do that for?" he demanded indignantly.

"So you'd shut up, naturally. If you'd mentioned Wonderland in front of that lady—"

"Mrs. Giuliani," Julie supplied.

"—she'd have known what we were going to do and told Mrs. Biggers."

"Or called the cops," Julie confirmed. "She did that last summer, when Lael was here and we jimmied open the Coke machine. We weren't stealing, we had the money, only not the right change, and Grandma's the one who collects it. She would have let us do it if she'd been home. Only she wasn't here with the key, and we'd been skating and were real thirsty and hot. Mrs. Giuliani is half-blind and a little deaf, luckily, or she'd be reporting somebody for something every few minutes: parking in the wrong place, or a water connection leaking, or music too loud. Grandma groans when she sees her coming. Come on, this way. Don't talk, so nobody will hear us, and move fast once I get it open."

We had gone out the back door of the laundry room into the late-summer afternoon heat. Somebody's radio was playing opera—the kind Ma liked, I remembered with a lump in my throat—and we were almost up against that tall gray wooden fence, out of sight of anybody unless Mrs. Giuliani stepped to the rear door of the laundry room to see what we were doing out there.

Julie cast a quick glance over her shoulder, then dug her fingernails into a crack between the boards of the wall. She shoved sideways and lifted outward at the same time.

A section of the wall—about four boards' worth—slid aside at the bottom part, leaving a tantalizing opening.

"Quick!" Julie said, and pushed Kenny through the hole as he gave a bleat of protest at being first into the unknown place.

She gestured for me to be next, and I followed Kenny. I was bigger; I had to scrunch down because the opening was narrower at the top and I sort of scraped going through. When I hesitated, because even though I was sideways it was a tight fit, Julie suddenly shoved me hard, all the way through. She slipped after me, letting the section of boards fall back into place with a rasping sound.

Only then, when we heard nothing from

behind us and I guessed Mrs. Giuliani hadn't noticed where we'd gone, did I look around me.

Wonderland.

The place was huge. Far bigger than I'd thought from the outside. We were standing underneath a section of roller coaster track that dipped and soared away on both sides of us.

Beyond, walkways went out in several directions, and even if the park was shut down, deserted, it made prickles of anticipation run through me.

It had been standing empty for quite a long time, but the paint wasn't too faded on most things, so there was lots of color. There were trees for shade, and benches under them where you could rest if you wanted to. And there were rides sticking up everywhere: towers, artificial mountains, water slides, and "mine" buildings built over underground tracks.

The booths were closed, of course, but the signs were still there: Hobie's Hamburgers, Wonderland Souvenirs, Westy's T-Shirts and Caps, Jose's Mexican Specialties, Suzee's Ice Cream Parlor.

We walked under the roller coaster, and

when I looked back I saw that it was a really big one, and high.

"Wow!" Kenny said, but he wasn't looking at the roller coaster. "I wish we had some money!"

"Nothing's open," Julie reminded him, leading the way. "They've taken the food and the souvenirs and stuff out. They put side covers from the roof over the cars on the Bumper Buggies, but you can crawl under the canvas." She headed for what looked like a big tent with a yellow wooden roof and lifted the edge for us to see.

"Maybe we could get the cover off," I suggested, peeling back a section of the heavy canvas far enough to display a bright blue bumper car.

"I never figured out a way to turn anything on," Julie said. "The main power's still on; the security lights come on about ten o'clock. But we can't make anything run."

"We could push the cars," Kenny said hopefully. And then, "What's that?"

Julie turned to follow his gaze. "The Splasher? It has cars that run down that steep hill and hit the water in the pool at the bottom. Only the pool's dried up. Just rainwater in it, and it's pretty scummy. Grandma says the heirs are idiots; they're not taking care of the place properly, so it would probably take a lot of money to get it going again. Mr. Alvinhorst—he's the one with the white beard who has the little trailer right across from us—says the rest of them won't let the granddaughter who wants to reopen it do that, anyway. They just want to sell to the warehouse people and get cash, and they don't care about the rides and stuff."

I put the canvas back over the Bumper Buggies, because there was too much to see to stop yet. "Where's that thing you played on, going to the moon?"

"The Moon Rocket. Over that way. Come on, I'll give you a tour," Julie offered.

It was no wonder she came here, even if it was just to look. There was every kind of scary ride I ever heard of, almost as good as Six Flags. The merry-go-round was inside a pavilion; there were doors on all eight sides of it, but they were closed now, so we could only peek in the windows.

"I wish we could get in," Kenny said wistfully. "There's a pink giraffe."

"I like that white horse the best," Julie said, her hands shading her eyes as she pressed her face against the glass. "The one with the red and gold trappings."

"I always liked merry-go-round music," I said softly, remembering how Ma had stood beside me the first time I ever rode on one of those horses.

"Me too," Julie agreed. "Come on, there's a train station over that way. The track runs all the way around the park, and in one place it goes through a tunnel."

We walked past an area where there were bright yellow and green and red and blue and purple toadstools to sit on, and some that were big enough to serve as tables. I could almost smell the hot dogs from the Tinkerbell Kitchen next to it.

"It's like Fairyland," I said. "Only the fairies are gone."

Julie nodded. "But it's still magic. See, here's the Moon Rocket. One of them's down on the platform, and it isn't locked. Two people can sit in it at once."

"Me," Kenny said eagerly, so we stood aside

while he buckled himself into the seat and began to manipulate the controls, a big grin on his face.

It was so interesting that before I noticed, it was almost dark. There were deep shadows forming along the western side of the wall that surrounded the park and inside the closed buildings.

"Maybe we'd better go," I said reluctantly.

"Not without going into the Pirate's Cave," Kenny protested. "We didn't see that yet!"

"It's dark in there," Julie pointed out, pausing at the entrance to that ride. There were little boats—gondolas, Julie called them—floating in more scummy water at the bottom of the canal that disappeared into a mountain of fake rock. "And there's no moving water to carry a gondola through. We'd have to paddle, and there aren't any paddles."

"We can use our hands," Kenny begged.

I looked down into the canal. There was green stuff on the surface of the water. "I don't think I want to stick my hands in that. Not in the dark. Maybe we can come back with something to paddle with, and a flashlight so we can see."

"An old broom would work," Julie pointed out. "To push us along. And Grandma's got a big flashlight."

Kenny didn't pay any attention to what we were saying. He ran down the steps to the dock and stepped into one of the little boats, a yellow one at the head of the line. It rocked but didn't tip over.

He reached out a hand to the fake rock and pushed off before I could yell at him to stop. By the time Julie and I got down to the dock, he was already heading toward the opening to the tunnel.

"I can see something in there," Kenny called back in excitement. "A light!"

"There can't be a light," Julie said, frowning. "The lights are turned off."

I stepped down into the red boat that was next in line, and Julie came after me. "Come back, Kenny. Don't go any farther in there!" I commanded.

"But there is a light!" he insisted. "Come see, Rick."

I didn't want him to actually get into the mouth of the tunnel. If he did, and kept going,

I'd have to go after my little brother. There was no way of knowing how long it would take to come out the other end—if we managed to get all the way through it just by pushing with our hands against slimy walls. Well, maybe they weren't slimy, but I felt as if they would be.

It only took a slight push to send our gondola close enough to the yellow one so I could grab hold of the back of it. "Come on, Kenny, cut it out. We'll come back with a flashlight later."

"Look! There it is again, and it's not very far inside! We can still see daylight behind us, Rick! And I can move just pushing against the wall, see?"

With that he leaned out and shoved as hard as he could, and since I was hanging onto his boat it pulled both gondolas inside the tunnel.

"Darn it, Kenny, I told you—" I began, and then my voice trailed away.

Because he was right about the light; I'd seen the flicker of it, too. Kenny pushed again, carrying us away from the oval of light behind us at the mouth of the tunnel. We bumped the other wall, where Kenny pushed again, sending us around a curve so that the light behind us almost vanished.

It was pitch black ahead. I heard Julie suck in her breath, and then the hair stood right up on the back of my neck. A leering pirate with a parrot on his shoulder suddenly loomed up to our left, an evil grin on his face and a hooked hand carrying a lantern.

It wasn't the lantern that illuminated him, though, but a flashlight, I realized as my heart thudded in my chest.

It wasn't a real pirate, of course, nor a real parrot. But there was someone real in the tunnel with us; when I heard the maniacal laughter I stumbled backward and sat down without intending to.

I wanted to shout out and ask who was there, but for just a few seconds my voice wouldn't work, even when I heard Kenny whimper as he, too, sank onto the seat of his gondola.

And then the light went out and we were in darkness, while the wild laughter continued to echo off the walls around us.

Chapter Seven

I heard Kenny's wavering voice say "Rick?" and felt our boats bump, then drift apart. I'd let go of the one he was in when I sat down, and I felt a moment of panic that I'd lost contact with my little brother.

He hadn't really meant to come far enough inside the tunnel to get completely away from the light, and he'd never have done it if he hadn't thought I was right behind him. He didn't spook about the dark unless he was alone in it.

I could hear the blood thundering in my ears as the crazy laughter died away, and then Julie spoke behind me.

"Who's there?"

There was no response, only the faint sound of one of the boats rubbing against the tunnel wall. I tried to calm down, because there wasn't anywhere Kenny's boat could go except on through the tunnel; there wasn't room to pass, and my boat was right behind his.

I wanted to say his name, to reassure him that I was close by, but my voice wouldn't work. Off to the side there were small scuffling sounds, and then a giggle.

Julie's words were sharp and didn't sound as afraid as I was. "Who is it? Who's there?"

The only answer was another smothered giggle.

"Is that you, Connie Morse?"

The flashlight came on, glancing off the fierce pirate with his parrot and his hooked hand, then settled on Julie's face so that she lifted a hand to shield her eyes.

"You don't have to blind me," she said. "What are you doing in here?"

"I been following you for half an hour," a perfectly normal boy's voice said. The beam of light swung over me, picked out Kenny crouched in the gondola ahead of us, then dropped so it didn't shine in anybody's eyes.

At first I couldn't see behind the light to

whoever was holding it, but at least if it was someone Julie knew maybe I didn't need to have a heart attack.

"Why have you been following us? And why are you in here?"

"You were heading this way. I figured there was a chance you'd check out the Pirate's Cave the way you were checking out everything else, so I ducked in here. Thought I'd give you a surprise. Didn't cost you anything, either."

The boy laughed again, only this time he didn't sound crazy.

"It was stupid," Julie said, but she wasn't angry. "Just like that stupid play you wrote for the sixth grade to put on at school. That's how I knew it was you. It was the same stupid laugh."

The flashlight dropped a little, and I finally saw the face behind it and realized why it had been so difficult to make out. Connie Morse— what kind of name was that for a boy?—was black.

"The play wasn't stupid. It was a fantasy," the boy called Connie stated. "I got an *A* for writing it, and another one for being the insane Dr. Murder."

"What are you doing in Wonderland? Nobody's supposed to be in here."

Including us, I thought. Kenny was staring at the other kid and didn't seem scared anymore.

"Same thing you are," Connie Morse said. "I been watching you for weeks. I followed you in here a few times."

"Spying on me?" Julie was mildly indignant, probably remembering how silly she might have appeared as she played she was going to the moon in the rocket ride.

"Well, you helped entertain me. Mostly, I really came in here to have a place to hide when my old man is drunk," Connie said. "He starts fights with my mom and I can't take it; when I say anything, or sometimes if all I do is look like I might say something, he belts me. One time he did it and I took off, didn't have anywhere to go. I came into the RV park to use the Coke machine and saw where there were loose boards in the back fence. I worked 'em open farther and I been coming here ever since. Nobody else ever shows up except you. It's safe. I go home after I figure my old man has passed out."

"Well, it's getting dark outside. Let's get out of here," Julie said, and I muttered agreement.

"Who are these guys?" Connie wanted to know, swinging the beam of light across us again.

"Rick and Kenny Van Huler. They're staying with their uncle, Mr. Svoboda."

"The old guy in the purple bus?"

Connie was crouched in a hollowed-out place where he was surrounded, I could now see dimly, by a tropical beach with a treasure chest spilling gold coins and jewels onto the sand. For a few minutes I'd forgotten this was a scary place for kids, and that it was supposed to be about pirates.

Connie suddenly slid off the shelf into the water, which must have been barely deep enough to float the gondolas. "Come on, I'll take you on the rest of the tour," he offered. "I'm Conrad Morse, only everybody calls me Connie. I'll pull the front boat, you hang on from behind, okay?"

So we got the tour. The tunnel twisted and turned inside the artificial mountain, and around every corner was a new scene on one of the shelves of "rock" on each side.

"When the park's operating," Connie told us as he waded forward through the shallow water, "there're electric eyes that trigger the lights so each scene pops up at you when you reach it. It's not as dramatic with a flashlight, but you can see what's here."

He'd obviously been through here often, because he knew what came next each time. He'd shine the flashlight on the pirates as they buried their treasure, and on their ship as they made someone walk the plank, and then there was a pretty spooky scene where everything was supposed to be underwater— there were fish suspended around the hulk of a sunken ship, and another pirate treasure spilling out onto the bottom of the sea.

Our guide stopped at that one, playing the flashlight over sea urchins and starfish and a corroded anchor so we could see the details. "When the regular lights are on," he said, "they have a greenish one here, so it looks more like it's underwater."

"You were through here when this place was operating, then?" I asked.

"Sure. Lots of times. We live over the corner

grocery, six blocks down, two blocks over. Our whole family came to the grand reopening, when they redecorated everything and built the new roller coaster, when I was about seven. Then the summer before it closed, my old man bought a family ticket for the season. Course he was drunk when he did it, and he didn't remember afterwards and thought I stole the money while he was passed out. He tried to get a refund on the ticket, but they wouldn't give his money back, and if I hadn't run off to my grandma's and hid out for a couple days he'd probably have beat me senseless."

Connie said these things offhandedly, the way I'd have talked about walking to the store for a loaf of bread, but it made me shiver. My folks had argued, but they never hit each other, or got passing-out drunk. It made me think of Ma being missing, and Pa going off without saying good-bye, and I forgot about the scene of the sunken pirate ship.

"Anyway," Connie went on, "I already had the ticket. So I came over here almost every day, the whole summer. I felt bad when they shut it down when old Mr. Mixon died. Every time the old man gets to drinking so it's not safe to be around him, I come over here. You want to see where I sleep sometimes?"

"Sure," Kenny said immediately. Already he'd accepted Connie as a friend.

We went on the rest of the way through the tunnel of the pirates; when we came out into the open air, right where we'd started from, it was dark enough so we couldn't see very far, but since Connie had the flashlight, it didn't seem to matter so much.

"Why didn't you ever say anything, if you knew I was here, too?" Julie wanted to know as we trudged along past a huge tower that had an elevator to take you up high before you got dropped in parachutes. She sounded sort of resentful.

"I didn't want anybody to know I was coming here," Connie said cheerfully. "And I figured you wanted privacy, too. Only tonight I couldn't resist the chance to spook you in the pirate's cave."

"Thanks a lot," I said, but I wasn't really resentful. Not now, anyway. "Where do you sleep?"

"Got me a good place," Connie said with satisfaction. "Not if it's too cold, but in the summer it's great."

He swung the light up and illuminated one of those Mexican hats that stood maybe twenty feet high; it had seats around the brim and gave you a wild ride when they turned the machine on and made it tilt and dip while it was going up and down and around in circles all at the same time.

"Under the Big Sombrero," Connie explained unnecessarily. "When it's turned off, it's not that high off the platform, but it's good shelter from the rain or the sun, either one. I brought over an old sleeping bag and a pillow, and I keep a box of crackers and a bucket of peanut butter there, too. Just in case I can't go home for a while."

Kenny had to climb up and look at the place close up. "I wish I could come here when everything's running," he said wistfully. I thought it was probably a good thing it *wasn't* running. It would have made Kenny throw up.

"I wish I could find the keys to the lights and the operating buttons," Connie said when

Kenny rejoined us. "The main power's still on. The security lights come on automatically, but everything else is off. Old Wonderland is really something when the lights are blazing and the music's playing and the rides are buzzing and whirring and whipping around."

I wished I could see it that way, too. "Even if you could turn things on, somebody'd hear the music, wouldn't they?"

"I don't know. Most of the people who live in the RV park are deaf."

"Not that deaf," Julie protested. "My grandma's not deaf. Mrs. Giuliani isn't, either, at least not very much. Still, it might be worth it, to see it going again. Even if we got caught and sent to Juvie afterward."

"Could we do it?" Kenny asked eagerly. "Make everything run?"

"Not without knowing how to turn on the rest of the power," Connie said. "And you need keys to control each of the rides. It takes two people pushing buttons that aren't even close to each other to make a ride start. Safety factor, so some dumb kid can't set it off when people are getting off or on, or don't have their safety belts fastened. There's lots of stuff you can monkey around on, though, even if you can't make the motors run."

"We'd better go home," Julie said reluctantly, "before Grandma wonders where I am. She thinks I'm over at Mr. Svoboda's bus, watching TV or something with Rick and Kenny. Once her own TV programs are over, she might come looking for me."

We started back to where we'd entered the park through the fence. "It almost makes me wish I was going to stay here awhile," I said. "This would be a fun place to come."

"How long you going to be here?" Connie asked.

"Only until my ma comes back," I told him, and the remembering took all the fun out of everything.

"Where is she? In the hospital? On a trip?"

The lump in my throat was painful. "No. She disappeared."

Connie stopped walking. He had the flashlight aimed toward the ground, but we could faintly see each other's faces above it. "Like, abracadabra, poof, she vanished in a cloud of smoke?"

"Almost," I said, and told him what had happened. "And," I finished, "the police say she probably just went away on her own, and will come back when she's ready. Only if she *could* come back on her own, she'd have done it by now. I know she would have."

"What're you going to do, then, if the cops won't look for her?"

"I wrote a letter to Pa, in care of the E & F Trucking, where he works. He's off on a trip, though, and won't be back until next Thursday."

"And you're just going to wait until then to do anything?" Connie sounded incredulous.

Julie had stopped walking, too, and turned to face us. "What else can they do?"

"Was me, I'd go looking for her myself. Do a little detective work."

He sounded so positive he made me feel awkward and kind of stupid. "I'm no detective. Where would I look?" I asked defensively.

"I'd start the last place anybody saw her."

"The last place we saw her was on the street near the deli, but we know she was at the apartment after that. She left my notebooks and stuff there. I don't even have a way to get back to the apartment."

"On the bus," Connie said promptly.

"I don't have bus fare," I had to admit.

"I do." Connie started to walk again, and the rest of us moved with him. "When my old man's in a good mood, he'll peel off a twenty-dollar bill for me to run an errand for him. It helps a little to make up for the times when he slams me into the wall. Tell you what: first thing in the morning I'll be over, and we'll go see if we can find any clues. Okay?"

My hopes had begun to rise, even though I didn't really believe anything would come of this. Connie wasn't more than a year older than I was, and what could a couple of kids do? "The police officer already looked around, and so did Uncle Henry."

"Well, the cop was the only trained observer, wasn't he? and he was convinced your mom just walked away because she wanted to go. So maybe he wasn't looking as hard as we'd look."

"I *know* she didn't abandon us," I said earnestly.

"Right. You know your mom better than the

cop, so chances are you're the one that's right. First thing in the morning, then?"

We'd reached the place under the roller coaster where we'd come in, and Julie shifted the boards to let us squeeze through. I'd never have found it by myself.

"Okay," I said. "First thing in the morning."

I followed Kenny and Julie through the opening, and the last thing I saw when I glanced back, before the boards fell into place again, was Connie's grinning face above the glow of his flashlight.

"We'll look for your mom ourselves," he said, "if the cops won't do it."

I don't know why, but right that minute it never occurred to me that looking for Ma on our own might be dangerous.

Chapter Eight

Julie couldn't go with us because she had to help her grandma with the laundry for several of the old people who lived in the RV park: they didn't get around easily enough to do it themselves. She did Uncle Henry's, too, because he didn't have time.

Kenny wanted to go with us back to the apartment, but Connie shook his head. "No, you're too little. This might get risky, kid. You'd be better off here, with Julie. You can help her fold up towels and stuff."

Kenny stared at him. "Risky?"

"Well, sure. If you're right that your mom was kidnapped, and we find any clues, don't you think the kidnappers are going to do anything they can to stop us from telling the cops about them?"

I cleared my throat uneasily. "Like what, do you think?"

In daylight I noticed that Connie wore jeans and a bright plaid shirt, and he walked with a kind of swagger, like Pa.

"Who knows? Depends why they took your mom. If it was for ransom—"

"We don't have any money," I blurted, feeling my eyes sting in the way I was getting used to whenever I thought about Ma. "Pa doesn't, I mean. It was one of the things they . . . argued about. Not enough money. Or how to spend what there was."

Connie nodded. "Yeah. My folks, too. My mom says there would be enough, if he didn't spend so much of it drinking. Anyway, kidnappers don't usually pick anybody but rich people if they're looking for easy money. So there must be another reason they took her. If they just wanted somebody to torture—"

"Don't!" I said quickly. I couldn't bear to think about a thing like that, though I knew from the TV news that sometimes such things happened.

"Yeah, that's probably not what happened, anyway. More likely she knew something about somebody and they didn't want her to tell."

That wasn't much better, because in that case they might shoot her, I thought; but I couldn't put that into words. "What could she know about anybody who was a kidnapper? She was—*is*—just an ordinary mother who works as a bookkeeper for a trucking company. She rides the bus to and from work, and she minds her own business, except for listening to conversations on the bus. Sometimes she tells us what people were talking about, when she thinks it was interesting or funny."

Connie nodded. "That's what I mean. Maybe she overheard somebody talking about something that was a secret, and they didn't want her to tell. You know, people sitting behind her on the bus, or something like that."

"Why would they be talking about anything that was a secret?" I wanted to know. "I mean, on a bus, where anybody could hear them?"

Connie shrugged. "Who knows? People do stupid things all the time. Maybe they were planning a crime, or they'd already committed one and were talking about it. So they followed her when she got off the bus, and took her away."

I didn't want to believe that. If they didn't want Ma to talk about something, they'd have to take drastic action, and that led back to eliminating her altogether. No, not Ma. Besides, I remembered. "Nobody followed her off the bus that day. We saw her get off."

Connie took a different tack. "Maybe somebody just robbed her—you know, snatched her purse, and when she started to holler, they grabbed her so she couldn't yell."

"Ma didn't have enough money to make it worthwhile to rob her," I said.

"People been mugged for twenty-two cents," Connie observed. "Nobody could tell by looking at her if she was carrying much cash or not. And those drug crazies are so stupid they'll attack anybody."

"You're not making me feel any better," I said. I hoped this wasn't scaring Kenny, too. His lower lip was sticking out.

"I want to go with Rick," he said.

Julie met my eyes; *she* understood what we were saying. "You stay here with me, Kenny," she said, "and after we get finished with the laundry we'll go back to Wonderland. Okay?"

Kenny hesitated.

"I'll show you the Wild West Village—we didn't get to that last night—where they had a shoot-out every afternoon and every evening— And the Golden Nugget Mine—we'll take a flashlight, because it's dark in there—and then there's something else you haven't seen yet. The rapids in Devil's Canyon—when the park was open you could go down there on a rubber raft. Now it's got no water in it, but you can climb up the rocks on foot, if you're careful."

Kenny looked at me, and I said, "It's a long boring ride on the bus. Both ways."

"Well, okay. I'll stay here," he decided, which was a relief. If we did get into any kind of trouble, I didn't want to have to worry about him. Besides, I felt strange about using up Connie's money for one bus fare, let alone two. "Maybe you better stay outside," I cautioned, "until it's late enough for Uncle Henry to be up. Don't disturb him. We'll probably be back before then."

I had a strong feeling that Uncle Henry wouldn't approve of my going back home to investigate, and what he didn't know he wouldn't get upset about.

It *was* a fairly long bus ride. Connie kept talking, trying to analyze the situation. Everything he said scared me more. Ma had to be all right, somewhere.

Once, when he'd mentioned a particularly gruesome possibility, I said in desperation, "Maybe we ought to just wait until Pa gets here. He'll know what to do."

"But he's not coming for a week, almost, right? A lot can happen in a week," Connie pointed out. "If your mom's in a dark basement somewhere, being tortured, you want to rescue her right away, don't you?"

"Why would she be being tortured?" I demanded, almost angry at him.

"To find out what she knows, of course."

"What could she possibly know? She works in the office of a trucking firm, adding up numbers and making out paychecks and stuff like that. It's a boring job. She wouldn't know any classified information, like if she worked in a place that made secret weapons or something like that."

"That's what we're going to investigate," Connie said. "We have an advantage over the police, remember: We know she didn't just walk off on her own, right?"

When we got off the bus, Connie said we should retrace everything that happened when Ma disappeared. We walked from where she got off the bus, and he asked me again about where she walked, and where we met her, and what the car looked like that had driven along the curb beside her before she sent us to Willie's for groceries.

We walked slowly, so that we could check the gutters and the sidewalk next to the buildings, though I figured if there had been any clues in those places, someone else would have already found them.

"The car, you couldn't identify it. You didn't get the license number." Connie said it thoughtfully.

He hadn't indicated I was stupid, but I felt that way. "If I'd known she was going to disappear, I'd have paid more attention," I muttered. "It was just an ordinary black car. I didn't have any reason to look at the license plate."

"I'll bet it was the guy in the car who took her," Connie said. "Maybe we should ask the people who live along here if they saw anything that day. It's only day before yesterday, and there's probably old people live in some of those upper apartments. Sometimes they sit and look out the windows, watching what's going on. Let's ask."

I was nervous about ringing buzzers and getting into apartment houses. Most of them were like ours: you either had to have a key to get into the lobby or ring somebody's buzzer and hope they'd release the lock and let you in.

In the middle of the morning like this, a lot of people weren't home. Nobody answered when we rang their buzzers or knocked on their doors. We figured they wouldn't have been around when Ma disappeared, anyway, because they wouldn't have been home from work yet.

"If they *were* home they wouldn't have been sitting watching the street," I said. "They'd have been fixing supper, the way we did."

At one place a guy swore at us and told us to stop bothering him, but everywhere else that anyone was home, they listened politely and replied the same way. The trouble was, none of them had seen anything, at least not until we got back to our own building.

I nearly skipped knocking on Mrs. Fox's door, because I knew she was almost always crabby. She complained to Ma several times about how much noise us kids made in the hallways. But she had a window that overlooked the street directly in front of our building.

My mouth was dry when I knocked, and she stared at me after she'd opened the door as if I were a fly who had just landed on the rim of her teacup.

I gulped. "Um . . . I'm Rick Van Huler," I began, only to have her interrupt.

"I know who you are. The one who always runs up and down the stairs. Never walks."

I'd run up them this time, too. I felt my face getting warm.

"I'm sorry if I disturb you, Mrs. Fox. I . . . I don't know if you've heard about my ma, she . . . something's happened to her. Day before yesterday. We don't know where she is, and we wondered if you saw anything. Out your front window, I mean. It was Thursday afternoon, and my little brother and I met her on the way home; she sent us to Willie's for groceries, and she came on home, only she wasn't here when we got here. She'd been in the apartment, though, because she'd left my books she was carrying. . . ."

A frown formed between her eyebrows. Mrs. Fox was a big lady, nearly as tall as Pa, and heavier. She looked dressed up, as if she was on the way out.

"I heard something had happened to her. Thursday afternoon, was it?"

"Yes. If you remember seeing her . . ."

She shook her head. "No. I didn't see her. But shortly before I *heard* you boys coming up the stairs"—she paused as if to make sure I understood that we had made too much noise that day, too—"I did happen to glance out the window. I noticed someone I'd never seen before get out of a black car and come up the front steps. I noticed because that's not a parking spot—there's a yellow curb marked plain as anything. That means Loading or Unloading Only."

"A black car. When we saw her," I said, my

tongue beginning to feel numb, "she was talking to a man in a black car."

Connie, right behind me, spoke up then. "Did you notice what kind of car it was, ma'am?"

"A big black car, is all. Not a Cadillac nor a Lincoln, I'm sure." It sounded as if those were the only cars she knew about.

"Could you describe the man who came into the building?"

"Men," she corrected. "Two of them. Both in dark suits. One of them wore glasses."

"Gold-rimmed glasses?" I asked quickly, remembering the man I'd glimpsed driving the dark car.

Her frown grew deeper. "Ummm. I think so, metal frames."

"Can you describe them?" Connie persisted. "Were they tall? Short? Fat? Skinny?"

She gave him a look that said he wasn't too bright. "Did you ever try to gauge someone's height when you're looking down at him from the third floor? All I know is they were both dark haired, and the one with the glasses was getting a bald spot."

"White men, though," Connie guessed.

"Yes. White men. Why are you asking these things? Aren't the police investigating? None of them has been around to question *me*."

"They say it's too soon. They think she went off on her own," I said quietly, trying to keep my voice steady, "and that she'll come back when she's ready. But we think somebody kidnapped her."

"Kidnapped?" Now the carefully plucked eyebrows rose. "In our building? Good grief! And you think those strangers may be the ones who did it? In broad daylight?"

"It was broad daylight when Ma disappeared," I confirmed.

The thought clearly made her uncomfortable. "My gracious," she said. "That gives me chills. Of course I only saw them on the front steps. I don't know if they actually came inside the building. They couldn't have, could they, unless they had a key, or knew someone who released the front-door lock."

"Or they came in behind somebody else," Connie speculated, "before the door could close. Like, if they were following Mrs. Van Huler, and she was in too much of a hurry to be sure the door locked behind her."

That idea gave *me* chills, and I swallowed hard.

"Is there anything more you can tell us about the suspects?" Connie asked.

I hoped he wasn't overdoing the "investigating officer" routine. So far this was the best lead we'd had—the *only* lead. I didn't want her to think he was being smart-alecky and clam up before we'd learned whatever she knew to tell us.

"No," Mrs. Fox said after a moment's thought. "They were just men. Not real young, not real old."

Disappointment began to seep through me. It wasn't enough to tell us who the men were, or why they would have kidnapped Ma.

"Well, thank you," I managed.

"You're welcome, I'm sure. I never had any problems with your *mother.* She seemed like a nice lady. Quiet. Never bothered anybody."

She was friendlier than she'd ever been before. "Thanks," I said again, and was turning away when she spoke once more.

"I just remembered something about the car, though," Mrs. Fox said. "I noticed it when it drove up, because I was outraged they'd park in a no-parking zone. People are always doing that, taking up handicapped spaces when they're not handicapped, parking where they block the rest of us from getting in or out."

"Yes, ma'am," Connie agreed. "No consideration for anybody else. What was it about the car that you noticed, ma'am?"

"The license plate."

My heart leaped, until she added, "I didn't get the number. It doesn't do any good to call the police and report a number unless you can also identify the driver. You can't arrest the *car*, you see, only the driver. If the owner says he wasn't driving it, and you weren't able to describe him, the police won't do anything."

"What about the license plate?" I asked quickly, before Connie could get another one of his TV-detective questions formed.

"Well, it was bent up so bad. A nice enough car, you know. Washed and waxed recently, I'd say. So the damaged plate looked out of place.

It was folded right up, as if they'd hit something hard with it, you know."

It wasn't as much as I'd hoped. But it was
more than I'd actually expected.

We thanked her again. When she'd closed
her door, Connie grinned at me.

"See? I told you we'd find clues. We've
talked to the rest of the people on this floor, so
let's check out your apartment."

I knew as soon as I opened the door that
someone had been there.

Connie knew it, too, and he'd never been in
the place before.

"Wow," he said softly. "Just like in the movies, huh? The place has been ransacked!"

For long seconds I stood there looking at
all the stuff that had been knocked off Ma's
desk, at the pile of coats and boots dragged
out of the closet and left on the floor, at the
cushions thrown out of the chairs in the living
room.

Even the police would have to believe now,
wouldn't they?

I wished I didn't feel so sick about it.

Chapter Nine

Somebody was sure looking for something important," Connie said, surveying the mess. "I wonder if he found it."

"There wasn't any money to find, if that was it," I said, picking up some of the things that had been knocked off the desk. "Whoever it was has been here since we came back yesterday morning with Uncle Henry."

"And they didn't break in," Connie observed, glancing at the door I'd unlocked only a minute or so earlier. "So that's another clue right there."

I guess I was in a state of shock. It was hard to think.

"What kind of clue?"

"Well, who had keys?"

"I did," I said slowly. "And Pa probably still

had a key. He wouldn't have done this, though. And Ma, of course. She had a key in her purse."

"And her purse disappeared when she did, right?"

"I guess so. We didn't find it anywhere." Ma wouldn't have made this mess, either, I thought, which could only mean one thing. "Somebody used Ma's key," I said. "Somebody . . . took it away from her. I don't see what good it does us to know that."

"It might be evidence the police would pay attention to."

I remembered how the police officer at the station had found a reason to dismiss every point we'd brought up. "Or they could decide somebody found her purse where it had been thrown away in an alley after they took what money there was left in it, and got the address from her ID and came here with the key to rob the place."

Connie was thoughtful as he walked around the living room. "Look at the way they took the cushions out of the chairs and the couch. They wouldn't have looked under those for money; people keep their money in better places than that. They were looking for something that had been hidden. The doors are left open on the record cabinet, so they looked there, too. What could they have thought was hidden?"

I didn't know. We walked through the place trying to figure out if anything had been taken, but I couldn't tell. Most of Pa's stuff was gone, but nothing else was missing that should have been there, as far as I could see.

I had to agree with Connie, though, that it hadn't simply been an ordinary thief. The TV and the VCR were still there, and the camera that belonged to Pa. Even Ma's best earrings were in the box on her dresser, the ones Pa gave her for Christmas a year ago. Those were all things a burglar would have taken because they'd be easy to sell.

We gave up looking any further.

"I suppose we'd better talk to the police again," I said. "I don't know if what we found out will matter to them or not."

We decided to go down to the police station right then to do it. I was afraid if I called they'd think I was some kid playing a joke, and ignore everything I said.

Connie had watched lots of movies, but he'd never actually been in a police station before. I was really nervous, because they hadn't helped when we were there before, but I led the way to the front desk and asked for the officer who had talked to Uncle Henry.

"Sorry, Sergeant Mulligan's off duty," the officer said. "Can you talk to someone else, son?"

I had to tell the new officer the whole story. He listened in the same way, asking an occasional question, making a few notes. When I told him about the men in the dark car who had come into our building, he started asking questions.

"Did you see these men with your mother?"

"No. Well, I mean, I don't know. I couldn't see whoever was in the car, talking to her. Not clearly. The driver had glasses with gold frames, though, the same as the man Mrs. Fox saw."

"Lots of people have glasses with gold frames," he observed, making another note on the pad in front of him. "Did you get the license number on the car? Did this Mrs. Fox get the number on the one *she* saw?"

I had to admit neither of us could provide

the license number. We couldn't give a good physical description of the two men, nor prove any connection with Ma.

"We talked to just about everybody that lives in the building," Connie told him, exaggerating only a little, because some of the people hadn't been home. "Nobody let the men inside, of the ones who talked to us. We figure they were right behind Mrs. Van Huler and came in with her, or before she could latch the door behind her."

"Um-hmmm." The officer looked at me sharply. "Are you sure the car you saw with your mother had a bent license plate, son? Sure it was the same car as this Mrs. Fox saw?"

I had to admit I hadn't noticed the license plate at all. So, as the officer pointed out, it could have been a different car that parked illegally in front of the apartment house. "Lots of black cars," he said, and I felt my eyes stinging; he didn't believe me, I thought. He wouldn't do anything even now.

We told him about the mess where someone had been searching the apartment. He made notes about that, too, and said when the other officer came back he'd tell him about it. "He'll look into it," was the last thing he said.

Then he got busy with a couple who came in who'd been in an accident, and forgot about us. Connie gave me the high sign and we left.

"I don't think we did any good," I said as we waited for the bus to take us back to Wonderland RV Park.

Connie kicked at a beer can someone had dropped on the sidewalk. "I don't think so, either. But that doesn't mean we can't keep on investigating on our own."

Investigating what, though? What was there left that a couple of eleven- and twelve-year-olds could do?

It was only a little after noon when we got home, and Kenny and Julie were just finishing with the laundry. They had folded it up in baskets and were delivering it around the park to the people who couldn't come and get it themselves.

"They haven't been into Wonderland yet. You want to stick around and go with them?" I asked Connie. "We can have something to eat first. I can make some sandwiches," I suggested.

"Okay," Connie agreed as he followed me into the purple bus.

It didn't look as if Uncle Henry was up yet, and he hadn't been to a store, either, so we had peanut butter and jelly again.

I was pretty depressed. I'd thought sure the cops would look into what we'd learned, but I didn't know if they really would or not. The officer had had an answer for everything we told him that made our clues sound insignificant.

Kenny came back with Julie about the time we were finishing our second sandwiches. I warned them to be quiet, that Uncle Henry was asleep, so we sat and talked in whispers.

Kenny had had lunch with Julie. He was anxious to return to Wonderland, but Julie said we couldn't go yet.

"Not until Mr. Alvinhorst is out of the laundry room, and he was just putting his stuff in the washers a minute ago. And we'd better go over there one or two at a time. We don't want anyone to get suspicious of what four of us are doing in there, or why we stay so long."

Kenny shifted restlessly, unwilling to be

bored while we waited. "I want to draw," he said. "I need some paper, Rick."

I glanced around, but Uncle Henry wasn't either an artist or a writer, I guessed. He didn't even have a desk where I could look for paper. I kept my voice low so it wouldn't disturb him in the bedroom. "There's blank paper in my notebook. I know I brought it along, because I intended to draw some more, and that's the only paper I had. Where did we put it?"

We finally found it under the edge of the couch. Kenny settled down in the driver's seat up front, then turned to ask, "Is it okay if I draw on the back of this?"

He held up a sheaf of papers I didn't recognize. I reached for them to see what they were, and I still didn't know.

"What the heck is this? It's not my stuff."

There were several pages of Xerox copies of some kind of forms, or ledger sheets. There were columns of figures on the right side, with a list of names down the left side.

I studied them, frowning. "I don't know how this got in my notebook."

Connie suddenly sat up straight, his face

alert. "Your mom was the one who took your notebook home, right?"

I turned slowly to look at him. "Yeah. Yeah! Maybe Ma stuck these papers inside the cover. Sure, that could be it. They're something she was bringing home, maybe some of her work. That's what she does, bookkeeping for E & F Trucking. She uses a calculator and adds up a lot of numbers and figures out payroll deductions, that kind of thing."

Connie stretched out a hand for the papers and I gave them to him to look at. He pursed his lips.

"These don't look like work she's doing. I mean, there are totals at the bottom; she's not still adding them up."

"She might be looking for a mistake. A column that didn't balance," I speculated.

Julie peered over my shoulder. "What are all the names for?"

I studied them thoughtfully. "Hmm. Names of companies, I think. Sure, they're people who had E & F haul stuff for them. That one, there, is the company that shipped the TV sets in the load that got highjacked. And I remember this name, McCallam Electronics. Pa hauls stuff from them all the time, and from Alvarez Plumbing Supply too."

"So the figures must be what each one was charged for what was hauled."

"Right. Just routine stuff." Then a thought struck me, so hard I actually had to sit down beside Connie on the couch. "Or maybe they're something important, something she stuck inside my notebook to keep safe. Maybe . . ." I hesitated, feeling melodramatic and half-scared. "Maybe these papers are what some-one was looking for in our apartment, though I can't see what would be important about them."

I could tell that Connie was getting excited. "Maybe she stuck them in your notebook to hide them from those guys in the car. Maybe they really are important, Rick!"

"But if they were important, would she have been careless enough to drop them on the steps?" Julie asked. She'd heard the whole story in detail, too.

"She might," I said slowly, "if the men were close behind her and she didn't want to be caught with these papers on her. It just looks like a kid's school notebook, with some graded papers in it. If she was afraid of the men, afraid they'd try to take the papers away from her, she didn't have much to lose by dropping the notebook. She knew we'd be along in a few minutes and find it. If the men found it first, it wouldn't be any worse than having them take the papers away from her."

Julie was sitting in Uncle Henry's one easy chair. Her mouth formed a round O before she said, "In that case, it means the papers are *really* important."

In the silence we heard a siren off in the distance. I felt prickles along my spine as I studied the papers, trying to figure out what could make them important enough so Ma might have been kidnapped to get at them. I didn't want to think what might have happened to her when they discovered she didn't have them on her person.

"Maybe the cops will believe *these* are evidence," Connie said softly. "Even if we don't understand just how."

"No," I heard myself saying. "No, they haven't

done anything about any of what we've said, so far. No, I'll save the papers for Pa. He works there, too; he'd probably have a better idea of what they mean than the police would. He knows how things are run at E & F."

Kenny had been drawing something on the back of another sheet of paper, not appearing to pay any attention to the rest of us until he suddenly joined the conversation. "Pa may not work at E & F anymore if they fire him."

"Why would they fire him?" Connie wanted to know.

He spoke a little bit louder than he had been, and I put a finger on my lips as I looked apprehensively toward the bedroom door at the back of the coach.

"Because he let a load get hijacked," Kenny said. "Didn't he, Rick? While he was eating supper, but he couldn't help it, could he? They unhooked his trailer and drove it away while he was eating, and they were mad at Pa for that."

An idea was taking form in my mind, still not clear enough so I could get a real picture. "That was what Ma and Pa were arguing about," I said slowly. "Before he walked out and didn't come back."

"I wish my old man would walk out and not come back," Connie asserted. "It would make it easier on the whole family. Except that we'd miss what he brings home of his paycheck."

"Ma asked if he'd had anything to do with the hijacking." I continued to think aloud, hardly aware of what Connie had said. "It made him really mad. I don't think he would have cooperated with hijackers, ever. He always told us to be honest, not to do anything illegal, or take anything that didn't belong to us. Once Kenny swiped some gum in a store, and Pa made him take it back and apologize."

Connie was thinking hard. "But what if he—your old man—really needed money bad? What if he decided, just once, to do something that would get him the money? Like taking a bribe to leave the truck long enough so somebody could steal his load?"

Kenny catapulted out of the driver's seat and threw himself on Connie before anyone could stop him. "He didn't! He didn't! Don't you dare call my pa a thief!"

I grabbed him and got a hand over his mouth, hauling him off Connie's lap. "Shush! Don't wake up Uncle Henry! Connie didn't mean anything, he's just thinking out loud, trying to figure out what's going on, what these papers can mean."

Kenny had started to cry. "Pa's not a crook," he protested.

"No, of course he isn't," I said, and hugged him. I figured that's what Ma would have done.

"I didn't mean your old man's a thief," Connie said, sounding apologetic. "But there's got to be some sense to somebody kidnapping your mom, and these papers make it look like it might be because of something she found out where she works. Your dad works at the same place, so there might be a connection between his load that was hijacked and the pages she brought home. See?"

Clearly Kenny didn't understand any of it, except that it had sounded like Connie was saying bad things about Pa.

Julie stood up. "Come on. Let's go outside and mess around until we can sneak through the laundry room and go back to Wonderland. Remember, Kenny, all the things I told you we'd go and see?"

Kenny had dropped my notebook when he stood up, and Connie bent over to pick it up. He started to put it on the little table beside Uncle Henry's chair, then hesitated, examining it more closely.

"What's the matter?" I asked.

"Look. There's a footprint on the cover. Not yours, it's too big."

"It got dropped on the steps, either by accident or because Ma did it on purpose. Somebody walked on it."

I took it to stick it back under the couch— there wasn't much spare storage space in the purple bus—and then looked at it more closely.

"Whoever it was had just walked in oil, it looks like. It made a really clear print, didn't it? You can even see the pattern on the heel, all swirls." I bent to slide the notebook into its hiding place and we all went outside before I added the thought that had come to me.

"What if the guy who stepped on it was one of those men Mrs. Fox saw? The ones who might have had something to do with Ma's disappearance."

"Could have been," Connie reflected as we started walking toward the Coke machine outside the laundry room. "There probably weren't very many men going up those steps between the time your mom got there and when you kids showed up. I'll bet it *was* them. All we need to do now is find a guy whose heel makes a print like that, and he has a car with a bent front license plate."

"Sure," I said bleakly. "And how do we do that?"

Nobody answered, and Connie started dropping coins into the Coke machine while we all stood there trying to figure it out.

If only Pa would come home, I thought longingly. I knew he'd take charge when he came.

Only what was happening to Ma in the meantime?

Chapter Ten

If it hadn't been for the nagging worry that hung in the back of my mind, it would have been a great afternoon.

I *almost* forgot the things I was worrying about. I didn't want to stay with Uncle Henry any longer than we had to, but I had to admit that playing in Wonderland was the most fun I'd had in a long time.

Julie had shown us a lot of things, but Connie was the one who had spent the most time inside the park, and he'd also been the most adventurous.

He lived in a part of town where very few other people lived because it was mostly warehouses and businesses like electrical and plumbing supplies, and various wholesale houses. The people who did live in apartments over little shops, the way Connie's family did, were older people, like the ones in the Wonderland RV Park. Connie's best friends were kids he went to school with, but they lived a long way off—too far to walk very often, and too expensive to visit regularly on the bus.

Anyway, I was glad he was with us, because he knew all kinds of things Julie didn't know about Wonderland.

He had been inside all the scary places that Julie had barely investigated from the outside. In the mine, for instance, we squeezed past the cars that needed electricity to operate and went down into the darkness of the underground tunnel.

We'd brought Uncle Henry's flashlight, Julie had one, and so did Connie; we flashed them around to see as much as we could of the inside of the mine. It was interesting, and we could stop when we wanted to look more closely at the exhibits of miners working with their picks and shovels.

Connie and I climbed up the bobsled track, which was solid rather than having a lot of open work under it the way the roller coaster did, so we didn't feel as if we'd fall through. The whole trough, which went up and down in steep slopes and tilted from one side to the other, was supposed to look as if it were covered with ice. It was really only pale blue paint.

Julie wouldn't go, and after the first incline, Kenny decided he wouldn't either. It *was* scary, because we had to crawl uphill on our hands and knees, and when I looked down from the top Julie and Kenny weren't much bigger than ants. It was easy to pretend we were mountain climbers in the Himalayas; I imagined an icy wind howling around my ears as I was poised there on the top of the world.

"Watch your step going down," Connie called. "It's trickier, so don't slip."

Going down meant hanging onto the cross-ties of the track even more carefully than when we were going up, or we'd have just rolled down over tracks and all and probably scraped off a lot of skin. It was fun, though.

And then I had the accident that made everything suddenly get downright exciting.

We were in a sort of dip, before the final hill at the end, and I stopped to lean over the edge and look down. The view from the top had been incredible, out over the whole park, and from up there nothing looked neglected or faded at all.

Even from down in the dip the view was pretty good, though I couldn't see as far. "When we get down," I said to Connie, "let's go climb the rapids, too. With no water in them, it should be a cinch."

"It is," Connie agreed. "I've done it a couple of times."

I hung a little farther over the edge of the bobsled-track wall. "What's that down there? I don't remember noticing it before."

Connie crawled over beside me to look. "Just a shed, looks like. I never paid any attention to it, either. It's not painted a bright color, so it sort of fades into the background, same as the fence. Where they keep tools or something, probably. I guess from the ground it must be shielded by the train station."

"Hey, Rick! Hurry up, we're going to go—"

I never heard the end of whatever Kenny was going to say. I turned my head to look at him approaching below, and I lost my balance and my grip on the edge of the bobsled run.

I didn't have more than a few seconds to get scared, falling over, and then I hit the roof of the shed beneath me.

I felt the shock of the impact more than pain; there was a racket of splintering wood, and then I was *through* the roof. At least part of me was.

Dazed, I sort of hung there on my elbows for a minute or two. Julie and Kenny had disappeared from view as soon as I fell, and I could hear them yelling, as well as Connie's voice from above.

"Rick! You all right?"

I didn't know yet. I twisted my head to look up and saw Connie hanging dangerously over the side of the run.

"Don't . . . don't fall," I managed finally.

"Are you hurt?" Connie's face was anxious.

"Uh . . . I guess I scraped a few places. I'm . . . sort of stuck."

I had a moment of feeling guilty—we were, after all, trespassing, and the possibility of an accident where someone got hurt was one reason the owners wouldn't want kids playing around in here. And then as some of the shock wore off and the stinging began in the places where I'd been scraped, I decided I wasn't really stuck too bad.

I tried to lift with my arms and raise the lower half of my body out of the hole I'd made in the roof.

Immediately I stopped. One of the splintered boards under the torn roofing gouged into my hip enough to make me reconsider how to get loose without making a real hole in myself.

"What's the matter?" Connie was still hanging over me, looking worried.

"If I pull up, I get stabbed. If I let go to try to break off the sharp edge that's poking me, or bend it back farther, I'm afraid I'll fall all the way through."

"Can you see what's underneath of you? Maybe it would be easier to just go through, and then come out through the door."

"The door's got to be locked," I pointed out. It was getting very tiring, hanging by my elbows, and besides, they both hurt.

"A window, then. Windows can usually be opened from the inside; they have a catch that can be unlocked."

"What if they don't?" I speculated. "I'd be

worse off locked inside than I am now."

"See if you can tell what's beneath you," Connie urged. "Then if it doesn't look like you'd get hurt on it, drop through. If you can't get a window open, we'll think of something else. Don't worry; we won't leave you stuck in there, Rick. I'm going on down to the bottom of the bobsled run; I'll be with you in a few minutes, okay?"

He was gone before I could work up a reply.

"Rick, what's happening?" Julie called worriedly.

I blinked sweat out of my eyes and tried to see downward through the opening I'd made in the roof. It must have been rotten, I thought, or I wouldn't have gone through it.

The important thing, though, was to get out of there.

I shifted my body as far to one side as I could, wincing at the renewed evidence that I'd removed some of my hide. At first I couldn't see anything inside the shed, and then gradually I could make out the splintered board that was poking me, keeping me from being able to get out.

I said a bad word I'd heard Pa say once when he blew a tire on his rig. Ma was right; swearing didn't help much. I was still stuck in the hole.

I gritted my teeth and shifted again, trying to see past the plank end that had me trapped.

With no warning, my problem was solved. Something broke under my right elbow, and I simply dropped through the hole I'd made, down into the shed.

I hit hard and for a moment lay stunned, thinking surely I'd broken a bone in my leg when I landed.

Outside, Julie and Kenny were yelling, but I couldn't get enough air to answer right away. It wasn't until Connie got there, too, that I finally managed to sit up and feel my leg. It hurt, but when I got up I could stand on it all right, so I figured it wasn't broken.

"Rick! Jeez!" I heard Connie exclaim. "I think he must have knocked himself out!"

I drew in a shaky breath. "No, I didn't. I'm just shook up. Wait a minute, I'll see if the window will come open and if I can find something to stand on to get out. . . ."

I finally looked around. There was only one window, and it wasn't very big, I thought uneasily. Kenny could get through it okay, but I wasn't sure *I* could.

It was a storage shed, as Connie had guessed; there were racks with tools hanging in them, rakes and hoses and stuff like that. I was still dazed, and for a minute I didn't realize what I had seen as I went to the window and struggled with the catch.

Connie's face showed up there as soon as I pulled the window open. "You find anything to stand on yet?" he asked, relieved that I was moving around.

"Yeah, there's a bench I can drag over here." I got one knee up onto it and then stopped moving. "Connie," I said slowly. "You know what I'm looking at? There's a big panel here on the wall."

He tried to look inside, but he needed something to stand on, too. "What?" he asked.

"It's an electrical-control panel. Circuit breakers, dozens of them."

"Circuit breakers? You mean, like fuses?"

"Well, if they go out you don't have to

replace fuses, like the old-fashioned ones. If you overload these"—I tried to remember how Pa had explained it once when I went into the basement with him after a power outage— "the juice goes off and the switch cuts off the power. When you turn something off, so the power drain is less, you can flick the switch and it's the same as putting in a new fuse— the power comes back on. Gosh, Connie, it looks like the breakers for the entire park must be right here."

Julie was too short to look in the window, but I heard her voice. "Can't you get out, Rick?"

For the moment I'd forgotten the problem of getting out, and so had Connie. A look of eager anticipation brightened his eyes, which were about all I could see of him.

"Turn 'em on, Rick. Throw some of those breakers, see what happens!"

"No!" Julie sounded alarmed. "You don't want to mess with anything electrical, it might be dangerous!"

"It's not dangerous. They just turn the electricity off and then on again," Connie said reasonably. "There must be a main breaker that turns off everything, but that can't be off because those outside security lights still come on. But everything else must be off. Try it. Rick. See if you can make anything come on. Are they labeled? Can you tell what each switch controls? Like the one to the Pirate's Cave? Or the mine?"

I was shaking, but I knew that though this was a much bigger control panel, with many more breakers than the one I'd seen in the basement of our apartment house, it was no more dangerous than that one had been. Pa said it was safer to throw a switch to reset a breaker than it was to change a fuse, and everybody ought to know how to cut the main power in their own house.

"Rick?" Connie pressed.

"Yeah," I said. "Yeah, they're labeled. But we can't see into the Pirate's Cave from here. What's closest? What could we see if I threw a switch?"

"No, don't," Julie was saying, at the same time as Connie said, "Try the carousel. I can see that from here."

I read down the list of typed stickers beside

the first row of breakers, took a deep breath, and threw the switch.

There was a silence, and then Kenny said disappointedly, "Nothing happened. There's no lights."

For a few seconds I was disappointed, too, until I realized what would make the difference. "The only lights that would come on when I hit the breaker would be the ones that were left on when the breaker was turned off. They probably turned all the lights off. What's closest, so you could maybe flick the switch right there where the lights are?"

"Most of them are probably inside, behind locked doors," Connie said. And then, "Wait a minute. I think I might be able to get at the light switches at the starting point for the mine ride, because that's all open, not behind bars or doors. Throw the switch for that, Rick, and I'll run over and see if it works."

A minute later I heard him yell, and Kenny give a crow of delight. Julie's eyes appeared again at the window.

"Hey, you did it!" Even Julie wasn't protesting anymore.

I threw the rest of the breakers on, one after the other, and scrambled through the window, so excited I hardly paid any attention when my sore places scraped once more on the window frame.

We had power in Wonderland.

Chapter Eleven

It was fantastic.

We couldn't get to things that were inside of real buildings, like the merry-go-round and the train station, because they were locked up. We talked about trying to find a way in, but Julie and I both insisted we weren't going to break in.

"We already broke into the park," Connie said, "so if we get caught in here, we're in trouble anyway."

"But we haven't damaged anything," I pointed out. "Except for the roof of the shed, and that was an accident. There are lots of things we can do to have fun that won't damage anything. Like go through the Pirate's Cave now that the lights will be tripped for each scene when a boat passes it. They aren't selling tickets, so we aren't cheating anybody."

"And we didn't exactly 'break in,'" Julie argued. "That section of boards was already loose. We just moved them to one side to make room to slide through."

I guess we all knew that wasn't going to save our hides if we got caught. But we weren't hurting anything. Wonderland was what my pa would have called an attractive nuisance. That meant things that would draw kids to play in them, when they might be dangerous. Like gravel pits, unfenced swimming pools, salvage yards. Like an abandoned amusement park that probably was never going to open again. Legally, Pa said, it was the responsibility of the owner to set up some kind of system to keep kids out.

Not that Pa would take that as an excuse for our being in here, though I thought it was the kind of thing he'd have done when he was a kid. Who could resist any of this?

We couldn't. And it *was* better going through the cave with the electricity turned on; the "underwater" scenes were flooded with greenish light, and in the other scenes we could see details better than we'd been able to with the flashlight.

We still couldn't operate any of the rides. "You have to have the key, and on any of the dangerous rides—the parachute jump, the stuff that swings you around or drops you from high off the ground—you also have to push two buttons at once," Connie said.

"Far apart from each other," Julie supplemented, "so one person can't reach them both at the same time."

That still left quite a few things to explore with the lights on. And I discovered, now that we could see, that the controls for water in the canals and miniature lakes and streams were not locked up; they were simply out of sight of the paying customers. When you walked through with lights on, you could find the valves easily enough.

Connie and I looked at each other over the first one we discovered.

"Be a lot easier to float through than to wade in that yucky water," Connie said tentatively.

"If there was water in the rapids, maybe we could go down them with a canoe," I added.

Connie grinned. "Let's do it," he decided.

It took both of us to turn the big valve, throwing everything we had into it. And then came the reward: Water gushed into the canal, and everybody let out yelps of triumph.

While the canal was filling, we tried to get one of the rafts loose from the track it was secured to on the Devil's Canyon ride, so we could go down through the rapids, but it wouldn't come loose.

"Darn," Connie said, exasperated. "What good does it do to have the water falling over the rocks if we can't take a rafting trip down?"

Julie studied the artificial rapids. "I think we'd probably get killed going down with a loose raft. Look, see how the track winds around, and tilts, to keep the rafts from hitting anything?"

Connie had located the control at the loading platform on top of the "mountain" where the stream began, before it plunged over the rocks to the pond below. "Here's the control button, right here, and the second one is up there. All we need is the key to turn it on. Where do you suppose they kept the keys?"

"Maybe someone took them home," I guessed, but Julie had a better idea.

"I think," she said, "they'd leave them in the office somewhere. I mean, they closed the park without any warning the day after Mr. Mixon had the heart attack and died. People came back later and shut down things like the lights and water and stuff. But why would they carry off the keys? They just closed up the place, and I think they'd have left the keys to the rides where they usually kept them."

The idea of having the keys that would make it possible to start the rides was irresistible. "Where's the office?" I asked, though I knew it would be locked, as the toolshed where I'd discovered the circuit breakers had been locked.

"The office is up front, by the gate," Connie said. "I've looked in the windows. But it's locked," he added unnecessarily.

We went over there anyway, to a little building that looked like a miniature castle, behind the ticket booths and entrance gates. "The parking's all outside," Connie said, pressing his face against the first window he came to. "You have to walk about a block, which is one reason some of the relatives said they shouldn't reopen the park. People expect parking right on the premises these days, and if Wonderland were new they'd never let it open without parking space right by the gate."

The rest of us looked in the windows, too. It was disappointing, because it was just an ordinary office, with desks and chairs and telephones and filing cabinets. As if she were reading my mind, Julie said, "I always feel as if I should see Cinderella at the ball in here, or the king and queen sitting on their thrones."

Kenny was stretched up on his tiptoes to see, too. "I don't see any keys," he observed.

"Probably in a drawer somewhere," Connie said. "Or hanging on a hook or something."

"Is there a different key for each ride?" I wondered aloud, pushing harder against the window to try to see more of the interior.

"There have to be a lot of keys," Julie said, "so they can operate or lock up each ride. I think maybe they're all alike. I mean, there's a master key that would work on any of them. If not, they'd be labeled. But there's no way to get in."

There didn't seem to be. We checked all the doors and windows, which were locked. Connie jokingly picked up a big rock, painted pink, from along the walkway, and made a motion as if to throw it through one of the windows, but then he dropped it back in place.

"Let's go see what it's like walking through the tunnel along the train tracks with the lights on."

We were so busy that we almost didn't notice the afternoon was gone, that it was suppertime, except that Kenny finally complained that he was hungry.

It was so late that I thought Uncle Henry might have gone to work already, and Julie wondered if her grandma would be mad at her for being gone so long. Only Connie shrugged at the time. "Nobody cooks a meal on time at our house, anyway," he said. "I'll heat up a frozen pizza. Come back tonight?" he asked, pausing after he'd turned off the last of the lights at the Big Sombrero.

"Sure," I said, but Julie hesitated. "Grandma may not let me get out again tonight. I'll have to see."

As it turned out, none of us went back that evening.

Uncle Henry had already gone to work, and Connie stood talking to me after Julie went home. He was still there when she came running back to us with an expression on her face that made me stiffen with apprehension.

"Rick!" she called. "There was a phone call while we were gone! A woman asked if you and Kenny were here with Mr. Svoboda!"

My heart began to pound. "Ma?" I asked, hardly daring to hope.

"She didn't say, but when Grandma told her all us kids were off somewhere playing, but she could call your uncle, the woman said okay but to hurry. Only when Mr. Svoboda got there, there was nobody on the line."

Disappointment was a heavy pain in my chest. Could it have been Ma? Who else would have guessed we'd be here with Uncle Henry?

"That's all?" I asked. "She didn't call back?"

Julie shook her head. "No. But maybe she tried and couldn't get through because right after that Grandma got another call, and it upset her a lot."

We sort of hung there, waiting, expecting the worst because Julie looked so stricken, but for me the worst was wondering if it had been Ma on the phone, if she'd hung up because she was in danger, if somebody had hurt her before she could talk to us.

"Who was your grandma's call from?" Connie asked, looking sober too.

"Mr. Mixon's lawyer. He said she'd be reading about it in tomorrow's paper, and he thought she deserved to hear it officially first." Julie gulped and looked near tears. "The court case ended late yesterday. The lawsuits the Mixons were having among themselves, about what to do with Wonderland. They're going to sell the property—he said they'd probably be in as early as the end of the next week with bulldozers and start knocking everything down—they're not even going to try to sell the rides or anything, just let some junkman haul away what he wants, and destroy the rest! And they want the land the RV park is on, too. They have to give us thirty days' notice to vacate, and then everybody has to be out of here!"

Tears spilled over and ran down her cheeks. "We only have a month and everybody has to move, and nobody knows anywhere to move to! Not that's cheap enough so we can afford it! Just the cost of moving anything but the little travel trailers is more than most of the people can afford."

I knew it was real trouble for the people who lived in the Wonderland RV Park. They were old and most of them were poor. Uncle Henry could probably find another place to park his bus, but it would be very hard for most of the rest of them.

I felt sorry for everybody, especially Julie and her grandmother, and I hated the idea that Wonderland Amusement Park would be destroyed. It seemed a terrible thing to do.

Yet what overwhelmed me was that telephone call. It had to have been Ma, I thought, to tell us she was safe—or that she needed help, and where to find her—and then something had happened that kept her from waiting for Uncle Henry to get to the phone. It scared me something awful, worrying about what it could have been.

I felt selfish, thinking about my own problems when Julie's and Mrs. Biggers's were bad, too. But I had to ask. "Would it be okay if I talked to your grandma about the phone call?"

Julie took a deep breath and wiped the back of one hand across her eyes. "Sure," she said, sounding so subdued that I could barely hear her. "Come on."

Mrs. Biggers wasn't crying, but she was clearly upset. She didn't tell me not to bother her, though, but sat down at the kitchen table with us kids. Connie remained standing near the door.

Mrs. Biggers didn't have much to tell me. Only that the caller had been a woman, she'd asked if two boys were staying with Mr. Svoboda and seemed relieved to be told we were playing somewhere, and then had agreed to wait until Uncle Henry could be called to the phone, though she'd urged that he come quickly.

"Only when Uncle Henry got there, she'd hung up," I said dully.

"No, actually she hadn't. There was no dial tone," Mrs. Biggers said, trying to concentrate on my problem for a minute instead of on her own. "She must have just dropped

145

the phone and let it hang there, because Mr. Svoboda said he heard sounds but nobody was on the line."

I shut my eyes. Had someone attacked her, if it was Ma? Connie wasn't the only one who watched too many cop shows on TV. I knew the kind of thing that could happen while someone was trying to make a phone call from a pay phone, too. Or any phone, for that matter.

Connie's voice was unexpectedly sharp. "What kind of sounds did he hear?"

"What?" Mrs. Biggers looked blank, as if she'd lost the thread of the conversation.

"Mr. Svoboda. What did he say he heard? Voices in the background? Music? Traffic? What?"

For a few seconds I didn't know what he was getting at. And then I remembered a movie where they tracked down the crooks because they'd called from someplace where there were plane sounds over the phone, and the cops figured out the guy was calling from near an airport. "Planes?" I asked, hope leaping inside me again.

"He didn't say. Just that nobody had hung

up the phone." Mrs. Biggers looked at me. "He seemed to think that it was your ma, and he was upset that something made her drop the phone. But at least if it was her, you know she's all right."

Or had been up to the time she dropped the phone, I thought sickly. Why hadn't she left a message with Mrs. Biggers, before it was too late?

My eyes met Connie's. "It's important," I said. "It might be a very important clue. It might tell us where she was when she called."

When the phone rang we all jumped. Then Mrs. Biggers got up to answer it. "Wonderland RV Park," she said, sounding as if she expected more bad news.

"Oh, Mr. Svoboda. Yes, the boys came home all right. They were off playing. Yes, they're here right now. I think Rick would like to talk to you."

She handed the receiver to me.

I took it gingerly. "Uncle Henry?"

"I guess we got to have some rules as long as you kids stay with me," Uncle Henry said, sounding the way grown-ups do when you've done something that scared them and then they find out you're okay and they want to kill you for scaring them. "I want you to be home before I go to work so I don't have to worry if you're all right."

"Yes, sir," I agreed, knowing Pa would have put it stronger than that. "Uh . . . Uncle Henry, Mrs. Biggers told us about the phone call. . . ."

"Did she call back?" he asked quickly. "Was it Sophie?"

"No, she didn't call back. Not yet." I thought of the time the phone had been tied up when she *might* have tried to call. If somebody hadn't *prevented* her from calling. "Uncle Henry, what did you hear on the phone after . . . when you got here?"

"Nothing. She'd gone," Uncle Henry said. "It just about had to be Sophie, though. Only female I gave this number to."

I could hardly breathe. "Mrs. Biggers said you heard some kind of sounds."

"No voices," Uncle Henry said. "Just a train, whistling the way it does for a crossing, and the dogs. Dogs barking."

"Trains whistling and dogs barking," I echoed.

It didn't mean anything to me, but Connie moved closer to me. "Big dogs or little dogs?" he asked.

I repeated that too. Julie frowned.

"How could he tell over the phone if they were big or little?" she asked.

"Big dogs have deep voices," Connie said. "Little dogs sort of yap."

I guess Uncle Henry heard that. "All sizes," he told me. "Deep voices, yappy voices. A whole bunch of them. Well, I have to go to work, but I wanted to make sure you boys came home all right. I have tomorrow and Monday off, and on Monday we'll go talk to the people over where Sophie works. There must be some way to get in touch with your pa without waiting for him to get home. I'll see you in the morning."

He made it sound almost like a threat—he was probably going to chew us out for making him worry—but I didn't care. He wasn't going to wait any longer for the police to decide we had an emergency, and he was practically certain the caller had been Ma.

"Dogs," Connie said thoughtfully as I hung

up the phone. "Where would there be a lot of dogs?"

"They have guard dogs at a lot of the warehouses around here," Mrs. Biggers contributed, but Connie shook his head.

"They have Dobermans or German shepherds. Big dogs. No little ones."

"Lots of people have little dogs," Julie said. "In any neighborhood you'd find both big dogs and little dogs."

It was discouraging. There could be dogs anywhere. It wasn't much of a clue.

Connie was still muttering, "Dogs, dogs," under his breath when we left Mrs. Biggers's trailer and walked back to the purple bus.

"And a train whistling," I reminded him. "He said the way it does at a crossing."

Connie stopped in the middle of the road. "The pound," he said flatly.

"The pound?" I sounded silly, repeating everything anybody else said tonight.

"Yeah." Connie was grinning. "That's it, Rick. I'll bet your ma—if it was her—was calling from the city pound. They've got all kinds of dogs out there, big ones and little ones. They make an awful racket. And I remember from when my old man took us out there to get my mom a kitten: there's a pay phone right in front of it. And besides that"—he paused to add to the suspense, then added—"there's a railroad crossing right behind it! There aren't any of those guard things that come down to stop traffic, and there's a train that goes by there right about the middle of the afternoon, and it has to whistle because there are no lights or bells!"

I hardly dared to hope. A lump formed in my throat. "Do you really think . . .?"

Connie's grin grew wider. "Let's go see if we can find her!" he said.

Chapter Twelve

There were still several hours before dark, and we went on the bus, using Connie's money again. I felt funny about that, but Connie didn't seem to care. I made up my mind to ask Pa to replace what Connie had spent on my behalf.

I was really nervous by the time we got off the bus. Because it was a weekend, the buses weren't running very often, and we waited quite a while for one. It was farther out in the country than I expected, and there were only two other passengers. Though Connie said there was a big subdivision farther out, where the bus would turn around, there were no houses nearby when we climbed down. There were only a few more warehouses and some open fields and an auto-salvage yard with acres of junked cars rusting in unsightly heaps.

There was a railroad track marked only by signs, no bells or lights. My skin prickled and I swallowed, but the lump stayed in my throat.

The pound was a big concrete-block building with a faded sign; behind it and along one side were runs for the dogs with high fences around them, and there was a pay phone right where the bus stopped.

"There're no dogs barking," I said as the bus rolled away and nothing moved, nothing made any sounds.

"Sometimes they get quiet when they're not excited," Connie asserted. "Listen." He stooped and picked up a rock—there weren't even any sidewalks—and threw it. It hit one of the metal poles around the fencing and fell inside the nearest of the dog runs.

Immediately a dog barked, and then several others took up the chorus. Several animals rushed to look at us through the wire mesh, but most of them were wagging their tails. All but a Doberman, in a cage by himself, whose deep voice went on for a minute or so after the others had ceased.

My chest felt so tight it was hard to breathe. Was this where Ma had called from? What had happened to her?

I turned back to the phone. It was one of the older ones that had a regular booth, not like the new ones that are open with only a roof over them. We stared into it, but it was just an ordinary blue booth with a ragged directory hanging from the shelf below the phone.

Despairing, I turned and looked toward the junkyard next door. "What would Ma have been doing out here?" I asked, wanting to cry and not wanting Connie to see me do it. "There's nothing she'd have come out here for."

"She wouldn't have come by herself, I shouldn't think," Connie said. He knelt down in front of the booth to look at something inside. "If she was kidnapped, somebody must have brought her here. Hey, Rick, look at this. Is it hers? Your mom's?"

He stood up, extending a hand with a small object he'd retrieved from the bottom of the booth. I reached out for it.

"An earring. Gosh, I don't know. Ma wears earrings, but . . . this is a plain gold hoop. I think she's got some like this, but a lot of women wear plain gold ones."

It made me feel strange and almost dizzy, thinking that maybe only a few hours ago Ma might have been here, might have lost this. Where was she now?

Connie surveyed the open fields, the warehouses, and finally the junkyard. "Everything's closed up until Monday, I guess. Let's walk around and see if we can find any more clues."

There was a fence around the junkyard, and the gate was closed but not locked. The hinges squealed when we pushed it open. We went inside, and I even called "Ma?" in a sort of quavery voice, but there was only silence.

In the middle of the place there was an office that was no more than a shed with a tin roof. We looked inside, where there was a table they apparently used for a desk, and a couple of chairs. Through a door at the back I could see there was a tiny bathroom with a toilet and a sink.

No sign a woman has ever been here, I thought, turning away.

And then I saw it.

At the side of the crummy little building a leaking faucet had made a wet spot on the otherwise dry ground. And in the middle of the wet spot there was a footprint.

Not one I could take for Ma's, but it made me suck in my breath, anyway.

"What's the matter?" Connie asked at once.

Then he saw it, too. He gulped. "It . . . it's just like the footprint on that notebook you dropped," he said. "Swirls on the heel."

"I suppose," I said, sounding strangled, "there are lots of shoes that have that pattern on the heels."

But I didn't believe it was a coincidence, and neither did Connie.

We both were convinced that the same man who had come into our apartment house right about the time Ma disappeared had been here, too, and not very long ago.

"I guess we better go tell Uncle Henry," I said hollowly, "and see if he thinks we should go to the cops again."

We looked around some more, but there were no more clues of any kind. No sign of Ma. When the bus returned, we got on it in silence and rode back into town.

I intended to wake up when Uncle Henry came home early in the morning, but after I'd lain awake until past midnight worrying, and then had bad dreams after that, I guess I slept too hard. When I did wake up Sunday morning, I could hear Uncle Henry snoring. He'd come in without disturbing us.

Kenny was still sleeping. Nobody moved around the park except Mrs. Giuliani, who was walking her ugly little dog. I ate a bowl of cold cereal and then made up my mind. I couldn't wait any longer. I had to tell somebody.

I thought Uncle Henry might be cross when I woke him up, but he wasn't. He sat on the edge of the bed in his underwear and listened while I showed him the papers we figured Ma had put into the notebook.

He studied them for a minute. "Don't mean anything to me," he said finally. "But if Sophie deliberately hid them in your notebook they could be important. We'll show them to the police; maybe they can figure out what they might mean."

He put them aside and examined the earring and the notebook cover with the footprint on it.

"You're sure it's the same kind of print?" he asked, but he didn't sound as if he doubted my word, only as if he were sorting things out in his mind.

"Yes."

"And the earring is like some Sophie has, but you can't be sure."

"Yes."

He made that snorting sound, though this time it didn't seem to signify amusement. "Well," he said, sighing, "I could have heard the train and the animals at the pound on the phone, I guess. I don't know if this is enough to convince the police of anything, but we'll give it a try. First maybe we better go have a look at that footprint, compare it with the one on your notebook."

Uncle Henry reached for his pants.

This time we drove out to the pound in the

purple bus, and it didn't take anywhere near as long as the city bus. I showed him how Connie had thrown a rock against one of the metal posts around the dog runs, and he nodded.

"Sounds pretty much the same," he said, and then we checked out the phone booth again. There was nothing more there, so we parked the purple bus in the driveway at the salvage yard and got out.

"See," I pointed out, "there at the corner, where the faucet drips and makes a wet spot."

But the footprint was gone. The water had continued to drip, erasing it. There was no longer any evidence whatever.

I felt crushed, going home, but Uncle Henry was only thoughtful. "Tomorrow morning," he said, "we'll get up early and go see if we can't find a way to contact your pa. There must be a way, even if he is on the road somewhere. Get the police to watch for his truck or something. And we'll talk to the police again, tell them about the footprint and show them the one we still have on your notebook. Maybe now they'll listen."

We went back to the RV park and had breakfast. We had my favorites, pancakes and sausage, but I couldn't help being depressed. I'd thought we had a couple of real clues, but now we didn't have anything, it seemed. It hadn't occurred to me to find a way to preserve that footprint, though it should have.

I didn't even want to go to Wonderland that afternoon while Uncle Henry finished his sleeping. Connie came over, and I told him what had happened.

"Tough luck," he said understandingly. "But you can't do anything before tomorrow anyway, right? So let's go do something fun."

I went along mainly to keep from going crazy sitting around waiting for Uncle Henry to wake up. I'd almost forgotten that Julie and her grandma had a crisis of their own to deal with, until I saw Julie's face as she came out of their trailer to join us.

"I guess we're all going to have to move," she said listlessly, kicking at a rock in the drive. "Only nobody knows where to. Mrs. Bogen was crying last night when Grandma told her the park's being sold. She has no family, and nowhere to go. Mrs. Giuliani called several other parks, but they're all too expensive for the people here."

Connie and I were silent, watching Kenny trying to turn cartwheels. He wasn't very good at it.

"Grandma called Daddy this morning. In Alaska. He said he'd try to take time off to come down and help us find another place, but Grandma doesn't think our chances are very good of finding a place to live that won't cost a lot more than it does here."

"Maybe you can go back to Alaska with your dad," Connie said awkwardly.

"It costs a *whole* lot more to live in Alaska. They have to fly in all their supplies, groceries and stuff, so they cost more than anywhere down here in the lower forty-eight. That's what Alaskans call the rest of the United States."

Connie shifted restlessly. "Well, things are crummy. For everybody, I guess. But there's not much we can do about any of it. Kids never get to say what they want, or have any power to fix anything that goes wrong. So let's go back to Wonderland and fool around."

I could tell Julie didn't feel like it any more than I did, though we didn't feel like sitting around being depressed, either.

"But we can't," Julie said regretfully. "Mrs. Bogen is sitting there where she could see us go through the fence. And she's going to keep on sitting there, calling around trying to find another place to live."

Connie got a sort of funny look on his face, but he didn't say anything until I asked, "What?"

Then he shrugged. "Well, shoot, they're going to level the whole place pretty soon now anyway, right? So it doesn't matter if you know my secret entrance. Come on, you don't mind walking a couple of blocks, do you?"

"You mean we don't have to sneak in past Mrs. Bogan? There's another way?" Julie demanded, astonished.

"I was thinking about telling you pretty soon," Connie said. "Before, I didn't know you that well. Now we're friends, so it's different, right?"

Kenny sort of dragged behind as we set off past the front entrance gate of Wonderland

and along the street until we came to the alley behind the far side of that high gray wall. Connie looked around and saw no one but us on the street, then ducked into the alley and trotted along with the rest of us at his heels.

We went the entire length of *that* wall and then turned another corner. Connie stopped after another ten yards or so.

We were in an open space between the back wall of Wonderland and blank walls of warehouses on the next street over. Even if it had been a working day, nobody would have been likely to see us from here because there were no doors or windows in the walls.

There was a concrete drainage ditch through the space between the buildings. This time of year it was dry except for a narrow ribbon of water that trickled out of a big pipe sticking out of the gray wall of Wonderland.

Connie stopped and made a gesture toward the pipe. "Ta da!"

Julie's mouth fell open. "You've got to be kidding! You go in through *that*?"

My mouth didn't exactly fall open, but I was startled. It wasn't a *very* big pipe.

"We going to crawl through the pipe?" Kenny asked. "Is it dark in there?"

"Not for very far. I mean it, it's only a few feet. You can see the light at the other end. Look," Connie urged, squatting down and pulling Kenny down with him.

Kenny put his face into the opening. "There's bars on the other end."

"They push out. That's how I found it, from inside the park. The whole grille can be lifted right off. From this side, you just push it out. I left it off for a while, but I was afraid Julie would see it and wonder about it. So I replaced it and went out the other way. Go ahead, Kenny. When you get to the grille, give it a push."

Obediently Kenny crawled into the pipe, not caring if he got the knees of his jeans wet. Julie put her hands on her hips.

"I'm not crawling through a sewer!"

"It's not a sewer. It's just drain water. Honest!" Connie scooped up a handful and held it under her nose. "No smell, see? Actually, when I found it there was no water in it at all. But now we've got water running inside again. I think this was mainly for runoff when they sprinkled the grass or anything overflowed or there were heavy rains. It just drains off into the creek."

Without trying any further to persuade her, Connie followed Kenny into the pipe.

I bent to look in after them and saw that Kenny was out the far end. "It's not small enough to get stuck in," I told Julie, and crawled in myself.

When I emerged on the far side, Connie was explaining that he thought the grille had been removed for cleaning after a storm when debris piled up against it. "If they were cleaning it when Mr. Mixon died, probably nobody remembered to come back and finish the job. I think the pipe's too small for a man to get through it, but they wouldn't have left it on purpose without fastening the grille."

I looked back and saw Julie's face at the other end of the pipe. "Come on," I said. "It's easy."

So now we had two ways in and out of Wonderland. And we had another terrific afternoon, except for when we stopped to think that in only a few weeks they'd be bulldozing the whole place, dismantling the Moon Rocket and the parachute tower and the Splasher ride and all the others.

"And I'll never even get to ride the merry-go-round," Kenny said sadly when we went past the carousel.

I was trying to watch the time, because I wanted to be home when Uncle Henry got up. We went out the same way we'd come in, and Kenny was so tired we practically had to drag him the long way around.

It was Kenny who noticed it first. He stopped and let out a yelp of surprise. "It's gone!" he exclaimed. "Uncle Henry's bus is gone!"

Not knowing what else to do, we followed Julie into her grandma's trailer to see if Mrs. Biggers knew where Uncle Henry was.

She was peeling potatoes into a kettle, and she looked tired.

"He went to the police," she said, dropping in the last potato.

"Why?" I asked anxiously. "Did something else happen?"

"He came in here to use the phone." She put

the pan on the stove and turned on the burner. "He called the dispatcher from that trucking company where your folks work, and talked to him at home. He was upset when he got through, and he talked to me about it."

"Nothing's happened to Pa, has it?" That awful tightness was in my chest again.

"No. That's one of the things Mr. Svoboda wanted him to do, to get in touch with your pa when he picks up his load in Ogallala. I guess the man didn't sound very cooperative. Just annoyed that your ma hadn't showed up or called or anything. So Mr. Svoboda said he was going to talk to the police again, see if they wouldn't try to run down your pa, wherever he is. Said it was too much for him to deal with by himself."

Mrs. Biggers wiped her hands and sat down at the table, facing us. "I don't blame him. I hope he can make the police believe your ma didn't just run off and abandon you. He says she's not the kind of person to do that, and somehow he has to convince the police they need to look for her."

She sighed. "I don't know, I'm sure. Since

they told me we have to move, I can hardly think straight, so I'm no help to anybody. Anyway, your uncle said he was taking a footprint or something to the police, today instead of waiting until tomorrow. How can he take a footprint anywhere?"

I was puzzled and anxious and excited, all at the same time. "He meant the one on my notebook. Maybe this time they'll listen."

"Come on," Connie said, pushing himself away from the door frame where he'd been leaning. "I'll wait with you until your uncle comes home." Julie followed us out into the tiny front yard, and we stood around awkwardly until Connie spoke.

"You know, I'll bet your uncle had the same idea I've got about all this."

"What?" Julie asked.

"Well, why would the people at E & F Trucking be uncooperative? Why were they so disagreeable when Rick called them? I mean, it's more likely that something happened to Rick's mom than that she just walked off the job and left her kids without telling anybody, isn't it? I mean, if she wanted to quit the job, all she had to do was say so. Nobody could stop her. And if they want her to do the paperwork for getting out paychecks, wouldn't she have one of her own coming? Why would she leave without getting it? Besides that, Rick, those papers you found in your notebook, they're some kind of clue your mom found to something that's going on there where she worked."

"Something crooked," I said slowly. It was a scary idea, that E & F was mixed up in something like they put on TV shows, where people get kidnapped . . . or shot.

"Could that be it?" I asked slowly, as a cold fear crept through me. "Remember, I told you my dad had a load of TV sets hijacked. Ma asked him . . ." I swallowed, because it was hard to say and I didn't want it to be true. "She said did he have anything to do with it, like leaving his truck long enough so somebody could unhook it from his cab, and he got really mad and they had a big fight. And then he walked out and didn't come home again."

"Did he—" Julie began, but Connie, who was facing the street entrance to the park, suddenly clamped a hand on her shoulder to silence her.

I turned to see what had caught his notice, and the air froze in my lungs so they hurt.

"Run!" Connie barked, and without conscious thought, everybody except Kenny spun and dashed toward the shelter of the laundry room.

Chapter Thirteen

The blood pounded in my ears so hard that Connie's voice, calling to my little brother, sounded faint and far away.

"Kenny! Come here and just act natural, like you're playing," Connie said.

Kenny looked uncertainly after us, in through the door of the laundry room. "What's going on?" he asked, which for him was acting natural, I guess.

"Kenny," I finally managed to get out in a fairly firm tone, "this is important, so come right now. And don't look around."

Immediately his head swiveled, from the back of the park to where the purple bus ought to be parked and wasn't, to the front of the park. His face was blank; whatever he saw, it had no meaning for him.

I spoke through gritted teeth. "*Now*, Kenny!"

He walked toward us, kicking a pop can somebody had dropped, then picking it up to deposit it in the garbage can near the door, the way he'd been taught. Ma had a real thing about dropping trash around.

As soon as he got close enough, Connie and I both reached out and jerked him inside.

"What's going on?" he protested.

"Did you see the car turning in?" I asked, wanting to shake him for being so slow when we'd tried so hard to make him move quickly.

"What car?"

I sighed and pushed him behind me, then maneuvered so I could try to see back down the road to the entrance of the RV park. I couldn't see anything up front, though, without showing myself. And I didn't really have to. I remembered what I'd seen when Connie had shouted for us all to run.

A black sedan had turned in from the street, and it had a crumpled front license plate. Just like the one on the car Mrs. Fox had seen out front the day Ma disappeared.

"Is it them, do you think?" Julie asked

huskily. "The men who maybe kidnapped your mom?"

Connie didn't waste time discussing that. "Julie, there's no reason they'd be interested in you. Go back to your grandma's and see if you can find out what they want, who they are. If we can, we'll wait here for you to come back and tell us. If we can't wait . . . well, you know where we'll be."

"I'll go out the back door, then, so they don't see me coming and realize I was with you a minute ago," Julie said, getting the drift even if Kenny didn't.

He was looking sort of scared now. "What's happening, Rick? Are we going to be kidnapped, too?"

"No," Connie and I said together, though my heart was beating its way through my rib cage again. I wished Uncle Henry hadn't chosen right now to go to the police; who knew when he'd be back?

I wanted desperately to see what was going on, but I didn't dare stick my head out the door. Connie, though, decided to do just that.

I started to stop him, but he gave me a look that proved he was calmer than I was.

"He doesn't know me, Rick. If he's the guy who did something to your mom, and now he wants you and Kenny, he's looking for white kids, not a black one. I'm going to pretend I live here and walk over to Mrs. Giuliani's trailer and ask if she's got change for a dollar. I'll see what I can see."

He strode briskly across the road, not looking toward the car, while I waited. Kenny tugged at my shirt, and I spoke without taking my eyes off Connie.

"It could be the guys who kidnapped Ma. Be quiet and do whatever I tell you. This could be dangerous, and if we have to run we'll go back into Wonderland and hide. It's important they don't see us, understand?"

His mouth was open, but he nodded slowly.

Out in the open, Connie paused as if to tie his shoe, then straightened and glanced casually in the direction of the office. Then he went on across the road and knocked on Mrs. Giuliani's trailer, setting her little mutt to yapping until she came to the door. She took his dollar bill and a moment later handed him change.

He came back, sauntering along as if he had no thought in the world except to put his quarters in the Coke machine just outside the door. He shifted so that he could look unobtrusively toward the front of the park and spoke out of the corner of his mouth.

"The car's there, and it's got a bent-up license plate all right. There's one guy standing on the steps talking to Mrs. Biggers, and another one standing beside the car."

The quarters jangled their way down through the machine, and he pretended to be making a leisurely selection before he pushed the button and got out a red and white can. Then he stood openly staring toward the car while he sipped at it.

"What do the guys look like?" I whispered, though the men couldn't possibly hear us from this distance.

"Just about the way Mrs. Fox described them. My dad's age, maybe. Forty, forty-five. Medium height. Dark hair. Yeah, and the one beside the car is going bald on top. They're not wearing suits this time, though. Slacks. The one by the car has a striped shirt, the other one has a white short-sleeved shirt and a tie. He's handing Mrs. Biggers a paper of some kind, and she's shaking her head. Like 'no.'"

"Can you see Julie?"

"Nope. Umm. Everybody's looking back this way. Guess I'll keep on pretending I live here and I'm curious. The same as everybody else. People are looking out their windows."

Kenny slid his hand into mine, and I squeezed it.

"I think they're arguing about something," Connie said, and threw his head back to take a long swallow.

It seemed a long time before Connie finally reported, "They're getting back in the car. I think they're leaving."

I didn't have any sense of relief. If they were Ma's kidnappers, it was just as important to know who they were and where they'd taken her as it was to protect Kenny and me from them.

"Why would they want to kidnap us too?" Kenny wanted to know. For once he had sense enough to keep his voice down.

Connie was still watching the activity I couldn't see. I was the one who answered.

"If they kidnapped her because of something she learned on the job at E & F, like about the hijacking of Pa's truck," I said, "maybe they want the evidence she took. It could be those papers we found in my notebook were important. And if that was her that tried to call Uncle Henry, when she dropped the phone before he got to it, maybe she got away from them and tried to get help, only she saw them coming and ran, and they figured if they took her kids, they could get her to give them the papers."

Kenny had his face screwed up, trying to sort it out. "What good would it do to kidnap us? Why would that make Ma give them the papers?"

Connie and I exchanged a quick glance, silently agreeing that it might not be a good idea to explain how the bad guys sometimes used torture of innocent victims to persuade someone else to give up evidence. Kenny didn't watch cop shows much; he'd rather see cartoons, or build things out of Legos.

"We don't know yet," I said softly, watching Connie's face.

A little of the tension went out of it now. "They're leaving," he said at last, and dropped his Coke can in the trash barrel.

"Can you see their license number?" I asked quickly. "The back plate isn't bent, is it?"

"No, but it's too far away. I can't make it out."

Across the way, Mrs. Giuliani came out with her ugly little dog on a leash and began to walk toward the office. Connie grinned. "Going up to find out who it was and what they wanted. In ten minutes everybody will know."

We didn't have to wait that long, though, because a minute or so later Julie came in the back door. She'd gone home behind the row of trailers on this side, and then returned the same way to be as inconspicuous as possible. She was carrying a folded-over rubber mat, and her eyes were very wide.

"They had a letter they said was from your mom," she told me as soon as she came through the doorway. "It said you were to go with them to where she is."

"Yikes!" Connie exclaimed. "They came here for you, all right, Rick."

I felt as if it had suddenly gone colder. "Who did they say they were?"

"The one who talked to Grandma said his name was Packard. They didn't leave the letter. Grandma said your uncle wasn't here now, and she wouldn't dream of letting you go with anyone unless he agreed to it. They tried to tell her it was okay, and showed her the letter again."

"Was it signed?" I asked. My fingernails were digging into my palms.

"I think so, but we don't know what your mom's writing looks like, so we couldn't tell if she wrote her name or somebody else did. They wanted to know which was Mr. Svoboda's trailer, and she told them he was gone with it, but it's the only empty space, so they could find it easy enough if they drove back here. And look what else."

She spread the rubber mat open on top of a washing machine and we all looked at it. "Grandma had just washed this off with a hose and put it down, bottom-side up, to dry on the porch. The man with the letter stepped on it right after he'd been in the dirt on the path. It's not very dark, but I could see it plain enough. Maybe this is enough to take to the police."

I leaned forward, breathing carefully. There on the smooth back of the rubber mat was a footprint that matched the one that had vanished from the dirt beside the shack at the junkyard. It looked exactly like the one on my notebook.

A slow grin spread over Connie's face.

"Bingo!" he said.

We were all smiling when Kenny spoke from the doorway.

"Rick," he said, "the black car is coming back."

Chapter Fourteen

Connie said a word I only ever heard Pa say once, when he stepped on a bee in his bare feet.

"They're not stopping at the office this time," he reported, standing in the doorway. "They're coming this way . . . no, they've stopped to talk to Mrs. Giuliani."

"She doesn't know anything that's happened," Julie said anxiously. "And she likes to talk. She may tell them she saw Rick and Kenny here after Mr. Svoboda left."

"She's waving her arms around. Telling them where the bus is usually parked, I think. They're coming on back here."

"Hurry!" Julie said, folding over the rubber mat with the footprint on it, carefully so as not to destroy evidence. "Go through the fence, Rick, before they get back here!"

She looked around for a place to hide the mat, opened a dryer and stuck it in there, and put an Out of Order sign over the dryer's round window.

"It's too late," Connie guessed. "If they pull into your uncle's space they'll see you before you can both get out of sight. Duck out the back door for just a minute, stay close to the building, and then when they turn in come back inside as soon as I say!"

It didn't work out quite that way, though, because the black car stopped at the door of the laundry room and one of the men got out—pressed against the outside wall I couldn't tell which one it was—and then the car rolled past.

I couldn't see anything except the blank wall surrounding Wonderland, but I could hear.

"We're looking for the Van Huler kids," the man who came into the laundry said, and his voice sent chills through me. "Two boys."

"Oh, yeah. New kids," Connie said, sounding perfectly normal. I wondered if his heart was hammering like mine, so hard he could hear it.

"You seen them?"

"Yeah, they were around a while ago," Connie said. "I don't know where they are now, though. Their uncle's gone right now. Maybe they're with him."

"No. The lady back there said she'd seen them after Mr. Svoboda left. It's important we find them quickly; their mother sent us. We're going to take them to her."

Oh, no, they weren't, I thought. Not if we could help it. I didn't for a minute believe Ma wanted us to go with them.

"If I see them, I'll tell them," Connie offered.

"Be worth a fiver if you could find them right away," the man said.

"Wow!" Connie sounded as if five dollars was a fortune. "Sure, I'll see if I can find them!"

"Good. We'll be waiting right here in our car."

"Oh, who shall I say is looking for them?"

The man hesitated, then said, "They don't know my name. Tell 'em a friend of their mother's."

"Okay. I'll see if I can find them."

"You live here, too, little girl?"

Julie's reply was so soft I hardly heard it. "Yes."

"Same goes for you. I mean, you find the Van Huler kids and bring them back to me, I'll give you the five-dollar bill."

If she made any response to that, it was inaudible. I heard the motor die as the car pulled into the space beside the laundry room. I waited, but Connie didn't give me a signal. Nothing happened except I heard the man on foot get into the car and slam the door, and then I smelled the cigarette smoke as one of the men lit up.

"I got that black kid looking for them," the first man said.

The other voice was different. Softer, better educated. "Money gets to everybody, Zimmer, if you offer enough."

Was that his name? Zimmer? I'd remember that, I thought, trying to breathe as quietly as possible. I eased closer, pressed against the wall, straining to hear.

"Everybody but the Van Hulers," Zimmer said sourly, and I quit breathing altogether.

"Van Huler will come around."

"The way his wife did?" Zimmer asked, sounding sarcastic.

"She'll come around, too," Packard predicted. "Once we pick up these kids we'll have more leverage. Relax. Think about all that money you'll have to spend."

"In Mexico, though. No way we're gonna be able to stay around here after this next job goes down. We'd never be able to trust Sophie Van Huler even if we paid her off and she took it."

"Think about the money. Everybody likes money," Packard said with exaggerated patience.

I'd had to start breathing again, and my chest hurt.

Zimmer laughed. "Even you, Packard, huh? Me, I been on the streets all my life, never learned a trade or nothing except jockeying a truck. Lived by my wits."

I made a bet with myself that he didn't have enough wit to live on very well, but I was still scared of him. I kept a hand on Kenny's shoulder, hoping he wouldn't say or do anything to give us away.

"But you," Zimmer went on, "you got a good legitimate job. Insurance adjusters get to dress up nice, drive a good car, live in a nice house. I live in the cab of a truck. Me and my sleeper, that's it. Anybody can see *I* need money, but *you* can't be hurting that bad for cash."

The man called Packard—I'd figured out now he must be the one with the balding head and the gold-rimmed glasses—spoke in a voice that barely carried to where I was hiding.

"You're not the only one who's going to have to leave the country, and it takes cash to do that. If Sophie hadn't stumbled into it, over-heard that tape and filched it before it could be erased, we wouldn't have come to the end of a good thing. Too bad we didn't find out sooner where Sophie's kids are."

Tape? I thought, confused. What tape?

Kenny twisted his head to look up at me, and I put a finger on my lips. I jumped when some-thing touched me from behind, but it was only Julie. Her eyes were big and scared as she stood beside me in the back doorway to the laundry room, listening, too. I glanced inside, and saw that Connie was gone, supposedly to find me.

Kenny's whisper wafted to us in the quiet. "What are they going to do?"

I shook my head to urge him to keep still. If

they said anything more, I needed to hear it, and I sure didn't want *them* to hear *us*.

The smell of the cigarette was very strong on the warm, unmoving air. There was a long silence, while my nose itched and I hoped I wasn't going to sneeze.

Finally Zimmer said, "I'll be glad when this is over. The whole mess is making me nervous."

Packard was beginning to sound irritated. "I don't think this is the right game for you, Zimmer. If you hadn't made mistakes, there wouldn't be anything to be nervous about."

"Don't blame me," Zimmer protested. "Blame Cranston. He's the one who got careless, who thought Sophie was too dumb to worry about."

Cranston! My chest felt ready to explode. Cranston was the dispatcher at E & F Trucking! What was going on?

"I never figured on kidnapping," Zimmer said. "It was just supposed to be simple, setting up to hijack some valuable loads and sell 'em, and let your insurance company pick up the tab for the trucking companies. You said you'd been doing it for years, and if we didn't get too greedy your bosses wouldn't get suspicious because there are always some hijackings. You said Van Huler was stupid, but he was smart enough to figure out he was set up when Bones bought him a steak dinner to keep him away from his rig long enough to give me a chance to get his trailer unhooked. If Van keeps poking around—"

"Once we get his kids, he won't poke anymore," Packard said, still softly and coldly. "You talk too much, Zimmer."

No, keep talking, I thought desperately, but it had already registered that Ma must still be all right, and that Zimmer and someone called Bones had hijacked Pa's load, and Pa was innocent.

"Nobody to hear us now," Zimmer said defensively. "Makes me twitch, to just sit here and wait. What if old man Svoboda can't be threatened any better than Sophie? Then what? Do we shoot him or what? You got money, you could run right now, but *I* ain't got enough to go live in Mexico unless we can pull off this next job!"

"You worry too much. Once we get the kids, the Van Hulers will cooperate long enough to let us snatch that last load, and you know what it's worth."

Zimmer was still nervous. "If we get caught, it's a federal rap. Kidnapping, hijacking. We ain't gonna have to kill somebody, too, are we, before we get done?"

Kenny squirmed under my hand and looked up. I shushed him again, and he subsided, leaning against me. Julie was rigid and pale, and I suppose I looked the same way.

"I wish that old man would get back, so we can squeeze out of him where those brats are and get out of here. I don't like this. That park manager saw us, and that fat lady with the dog. They know what we look like. They can give a description if the cops come looking for us." Zimmer sounded as if he were chewing his fingernails.

"Why would they? The Van Hulers aren't going to call in the cops while we've got their kids. Neither is the old man. Now shut up, will you?"

They lapsed into silence that was even worse than what they'd been saying.

My mind was racing, and I was sweating,

trying to sort out what we'd heard. Somebody named Bones had diverted Pa's attention from his truck while Zimmer did the actual hijacking. I was confused and scared.

We didn't dare move. The panel that could be swung aside in the fence was so close, yet if we tried to get to it the men would see us. There was nowhere to go in the other direction except onto the street, and if they caught sight of us out there we'd be sitting ducks.

Connie's voice made us jump. He must have gone past the front door of the laundry room without our seeing him.

"Hey, Mr. Zimmer!" It was so loud that it scared me, until I realized who it was. "I found those kids! I mean, I saw them, but they're too far down the street for me to catch up with them. They're probably going over to the bus stop to go to the movies downtown or something."

"Where?" Zimmer demanded, and the ignition of the black sedan was turned on, so it drowned out everything except Connie's reply.

"They went that way, turned left out of the park here. The bus stop's three blocks over that way. You might catch them before the bus picks them up."

A moment later the men were gone, and Connie bounded around the corner.

"Now!" he greeted us. "Run!"

A few seconds after that, we were scrambling through the fence into Wonderland.

Chapter Fifteen

Kenny fell going through the opening in the fence, and he was sitting on the ground, trying to get his pants leg up to examine one knee. I struggled to get my breathing under control; I was gasping so I was afraid they'd hear from the other side of the fence if anyone got close enough.

Connie and I had been making guesses about what had happened to Ma, but I was stunned at what I'd overheard confirmed a few minutes ago.

Ma was still alive, but I didn't know if they'd hurt her or not. A driver called Bones had kept Pa away from his truck so the man called Zimmer could steal his load. It had sounded like it had been set up by the other man, Packard, who was an adjuster for E & F's insurance carrier, working with the dispatcher, Bob Cranston. They'd been setting up hijackings, with other companies as well as E & F, and somehow Ma found out.

Not only that, they were planning a big job and they were afraid my folks were going to spoil it unless they took Kenny and me hostage to force them not to go to the police.

I felt like I'd fallen into a cement mixer and I was tumbling around inside it, my thoughts all mixed up.

Cranston had acted like he blamed Pa for leaving his rig unattended long enough for someone to get away with his trailer, when all the time he knew it had been a setup. He knew who stole it and that Pa was innocent, and he himself was getting part of the money when they sold a semi-load of new TVs.

And I had sent my note to Pa, care of E & F Trucking, telling him we were with Uncle Henry at the Wonderland RV Park. Pa wouldn't even get the letter, I thought sickly, because Cranston had intercepted it. That's how these men had known where to come looking for us, that and Uncle Henry's call to Cranston this morning.

I sat beside Kenny, looking at the scraped place on his knee that was oozing a little blood. "It isn't serious," I assured him. "It'll stop hurting soon, and get a scab on it, and it'll be okay."

I wasn't thinking about his knee, though. I was thinking how mad Pa had been when Ma asked if he had anything to do with the hijacking. Maybe she was sorry she'd doubted his honesty and she'd gone looking for proof as to what had actually happened. Or maybe she'd stumbled accidentally on some evidence that it was an inside job. If Ma had overheard a careless exchange of words between Cranston and any of the others that made her suspicious, she'd have been looking for the truth, I was pretty sure of that.

I was convinced by now that the papers she'd stuck in my notebook had been hidden there because the men who wanted them were right behind her; would they help prove Pa was innocent of the hijacking and that someone else was guilty? And what was this about a tape that was missing? They believed that Ma had taken it, and it was evidence against them.

Something hit the other side of the fence

hard, jerking me out of my speculations. Kenny forgot his knee, staring at the gray painted boards only a few feet away, as we heard Connie suck in a breath. "Hey, let go of me!"

"You little creep," Zimmer said, and the menace in his tone was enough to give me goose bumps. "Thought you'd put one over on me, did you, sending me on a wild-goose chase after those kids? Where are they really?"

This time I didn't have to warn Kenny to keep still. His eyes were big and his mouth was open. He'd understood enough of what had happened in the past few minutes to realize that Zimmer and Packard were bad guys.

It sounded as if Zimmer had hold of Connie and was slamming him against the fence.

"How should I know where they are?" Connie protested when the thumping stopped. "They ran away, that's all."

"Yeah, and you helped them and you know where they went." Slam, thump. "And you better tell me quick, you little brat, before I bash your head in!"

"I don't know!" Connie howled, and I hoped it wasn't hurting as much as it sounded like it was.

I got to my feet and pulled Kenny up with me, wondering wildly where to go to hide. Connie was going to have to confess we were in Wonderland or Zimmer might kill him.

This time I actually saw the fence shake under the blow, and Connie's yell definitely was one of pain as well as rage.

"Where are they? I'm not fooling around with you any longer, kid, so you better tell me! They never went out on the street at all! Now, you want some more or are you going to tell me where they are?"

"What do you think, I've got them stashed in a cave or something?" Connie demanded. "Look around the park! They're gone!"

Again the fence vibrated under the power of a blow, and Connie cried out, "Run, Rick!" I grabbed Kenny's hand and ran.

Cave, Connie had said. All right, we'd go to the Pirate's Cave. He'd have to tell them we were inside Wonderland, but it would take them a while to find us. We knew our way around, and Zimmer didn't.

The trouble with the cave, though, was that two men could easily trap us there. You went in one end of the tunnel and came out the other end in the same place. Besides, it was too far away, I decided. We needed to get out of sight quick, preferably somewhere we had a chance of getting out.

The drainage pipe, I thought, but that was too far away if they broke through the fence before we got all the way across the park. And where would we go when we came out the other end? There was nowhere to hide beyond the walls of Wonderland; there were only windowless warehouses, locked up, no one working there today. No telephones, no people, and on a Sunday, no traffic.

We were probably safer staying here, if we could pick a good place.

Behind us, as we ran silently across a grassy patch, I heard Connie scream.

What had Zimmer done to him?

The places that would have offered the most concealment, real buildings, were locked up. Was there any chance the telephone in the office was still working?

I headed for that, and when we got there I didn't hesitate to grab the rock Connie had jokingly threatened to put through a window. Wonderland was being razed, and as far as I knew Kenny and I were in a life-and-death situation; it wasn't a matter of vandalism now.

The rock bounced off the office window in the pretty little castle the first time, leaving only a single crack from side to side. I threw the rock again, as hard as I could, and this time there was a satisfying crash. "Wait here," I told Kenny, and knocked loose the splinters before I climbed through the broken window.

It only took a moment to determine that the telephone had been disconnected. No calling the police, then. I looked around for a hiding place.

"Rick!" Kenny's face appeared at the window I'd broken. "I think they're coming."

There was nowhere to hide in here, I thought grimly. Only that tiny bathroom, with a door so flimsy it would never keep Zimmer out if he wanted to come in. He'd just kick it down.

I slid back over the windowsill, wincing when I raked my arm across a splinter of glass I hadn't removed, and I heard them.

"They're in here somewhere," Zimmer growled from not far away, "and you're going to show me where."

I spun frantically, jerking Kenny with me. The nearest thing to us was the Bumper Buggy ride, with the canvas tarp draped from the wooden roof, hanging nearly to the ground. We dove for it, wriggling under the tarp, and collapsed in the near-darkness there. My heart was making so much noise it was all I could do to hear anything outside for a minute or so.

"You broke my arm," Connie accused loudly, not more than a few yards away, after I'd begun to hope he'd led Zimmer in a different direction.

"Tough. I'll break the other one," Zimmer told him angrily, "if I don't catch up with the Van Huler kids in short order. Where are they?"

We were lying flat on the base of the Bumper Buggy area. There was a blue car on one side of me, a red one on the other side. Kenny drew in a whimpering breath. "Are they going to kill us, Rick?" he whispered.

I didn't have enough wind to reply. I began

to squirm around so I could look out, and found that I could see their legs, Zimmer's and Connie's. I hoped Connie didn't really have a broken arm.

Cautiously, I edged between a pair of the bumper cars, hoping to get far enough inside the layout so that if Zimmer squatted down and peered under the canvas I wouldn't be in sight. "Follow me," I whispered, and took it for granted that Kenny was coming along behind me.

The first I knew that he wasn't was when I heard him sneeze.

I turned my head so fast I bumped it on the corner of a car. For a few seconds I was stunned. I could hardly see, and then what happened made my heart stop.

Zimmer reached under the edge of the canvas tarp and caught hold of Kenny and hauled him out.

Kenny kicked and screamed and I think bit Zimmer's hand, but the man held on. He couldn't hold on to a fighting Kenny and Connie at the same time, though. Connie jerked free and fled in the direction we'd come from, maybe with the same hope I'd had, that the telephone in the office might still be working.

Or maybe he'd go back through the fence and call the cops from Mrs. Bigger's trailer, I thought hopefully. My little brother was being subdued by that thug of a Zimmer, and Connie was our best hope.

Almost at once, though, that hope died. I heard Packard's voice. They were both here.

"Good! You got one. Where's the other one?"

"He can't be far away. He wouldn't have left the little one. Shall we settle for him? Sophie's going to cave in if we start pulling this one apart."

I felt sick to my stomach, and helpless to do anything to save Kenny.

"I don't know why I thought you'd be any use to me," Packard said coldly, "except for your ability to unhook a trailer and hook it up to another cab. Where's your brain? We going to let the bigger one run loose and sick the cops on us before we can persuade Sophie it's too dangerous to tell what she knows?"

"They don't know where we got Sophie," Zimmer said, sounding a bit uncertain.

"No, but we don't want the cops nosing into this at all, do we? Give me this one, and I'll guard the hole in the fence so they can't get back out. You find the other one. Fast!"

Kenny was crying, but he hung limp, now, allowing himself to be handed over to Packard. Zimmer stood staring after them, swearing under his breath. "Find him fast!" he muttered angrily. "Sure! How?"

At first the sounds I heard behind me didn't register. I was concentrating on watching Zimmer, or what I could see of him between the bumper cars. He didn't seem to be able to decide which direction to go, but almost as I thought that, he took a step toward me.

"Well, the little one was under that tarp. Let's take it off and see if the bigger rat is in the same hole," he said, practically snarling.

I backed farther from the opening where we'd crawled in, and he started jerking back the heavy canvas.

I heard the sounds again, then, and twisted my head to look behind me, opposite where Zimmer was going to peel me out like taking the skin off an onion. The bumper cars didn't offer much to hide behind by themselves, once he got the tarp pulled off.

Was there a third man coming up on me from the rear?

There was somebody else, all right, but I felt a surge of hope when I recognized Connie.

He put a finger on his lips and lifted something I couldn't make out. Then he made gestures, but it wasn't until I heard the faint jangle of metal on metal that I realized what he had.

He'd gone to the castle-office, all right, and found the broken window and the dead phone. But he'd taken time to look further, and he'd found keys.

I wasn't sure what good it was going to do us, not with Packard having Kenny and guarding the hole in the fence so nobody could go for help, but I felt better knowing I wasn't alone. Connie was here, and he had an idea.

Zimmer was making enough rasping sounds turning back the canvas, cursing when it caught and wouldn't pull free, that he didn't hear that slight rattle of the keys.

I crawled rapidly toward Connie, and he put

his mouth right up to my ear to whisper his plan. For a moment I gaped at him, then nodded and began to crawl again as Connie retreated, keeping low so Zimmer wouldn't see him.

My pursuer gave a grunt of satisfaction at last as he pulled off one end of the tarp. I felt nakedly exposed as half the Bumper Buggies were suddenly in daylight, but I tried to ignore Zimmer and follow Connie's plan.

I dove for the pole where I pushed one button at the same time as Connie hit the other one; he'd already used the key to turn on the electricity that powered the little cars through whips that reached to its source in the ceiling. It only took seconds, and I was in the nearest buggy by the time I heard Zimmer bellow. He'd seen us.

Connie's arm had been hurt, but it obviously wasn't broken, because he was using it. He dove for a buggy, too—he had a yellow one and mine was orange—and we slammed down on the pedals and headed straight for our enemy.

Zimmer was threading his way between stalled buggies all over the place, starting to grin, before he realized what we were going to do.

The grin slid off his face just before Connie's buggy slammed into him.

It had rubber bumpers, but they were hard enough to hurt when they hit. Zimmer was thrown off balance, and then my buggy knocked him sideways. We quickly reversed and hit him again before he could get up. Then we abandoned the buggies and ran.

Zimmer was hurt, though not seriously enough to matter. He was cursing and fighting his way free of the bumper buggies before we had any chance to get out of his sight.

"The Splasher," Connie gasped as we pelted away, and I didn't waste breath responding.

It was only when we reached the top of the ramp where we were to board the cars for the Splasher that it dawned on me.

"We can't push both buttons at once and get into a car before it starts!" I cried, looking back to see Zimmer gaining on us.

Connie was already sticking the key in the lock beside the first control button. He was puffing from the exertion. "Jump in, and I'll follow you if I have time to get the next car. Anyway, after we hit the water, we'll split up. I'll go left, you go right, okay?"

There wasn't time for more. I fell into the first car poised at the top of the slope over the pond, bumping an elbow painfully, then looked back.

Connie had punched the second button, and the line of cars started to move. He dove toward the track and made it into the fourth car back.

Far off across the park, by the hole in the fence, I saw Packard and Kenny, who was so limp I was afraid Packard had knocked him out.

We were picking up speed when I looked back for the last time and saw Zimmer barely make it into the rear car.

And then the front one went over the edge, plunging down toward the pond below. I hadn't had time to fasten the bar in front of me, and I hung onto one side of the car to keep from being pitched out before we got that far.

Chapter Sixteen

When we hit the water it rose in a heavy spray all around our cars.

I almost fell in the pond in my hurry to get out of the car before it had quite reached the unloading dock.

I didn't look back this time, but headed right, as Connie had instructed. Within seconds I heard his feet pounding on the dock behind me, and I ran for all I was worth.

I knew who Zimmer would follow. It was me he wanted, not Connie, though no doubt they planned to catch him too, after I was in their grasp. At the very least, they'd keep him trapped inside Wonderland so he couldn't go to the police until they'd used Kenny and me to force Ma to do what they wanted.

Of course Zimmer didn't know about the

drainpipe. Even if he noticed it, he'd see only a grille that would presumably keep anybody out of it, and it wouldn't mean anything to him.

On the way down the Splasher, waiting for the water to soak me when I hit, I'd tried to plan. That isn't easy when your mind is racing around in circles and you're scared stiff. I tried not to think about how Kenny must be feeling.

My best bet, I decided, was the Pirate's Cave, after all. Zimmer could keep me cornered in there by simply standing on the loading and unloading platform, but if Packard stayed over by the hole in the fence, *he* couldn't help get me out. If Zimmer left to get help, he'd have to leave the exit to the cave unguarded, and he wouldn't be able to see which way I went.

Even if he ran to get Packard, I figured I could get out the drainpipe before he knew where I'd gone.

I didn't have a key to anything at the cave, but the gondolas just went through by themselves anyway, because the water kept circulating, round and round. I jumped in the first one and pushed off.

I didn't relish going into the dark, with no flashlight and by myself, but I didn't know what else to do. I couldn't tell if Zimmer was hot on my heels, seeing where I went, but I didn't have any other choices anyway.

Just as the little boat reached the entrance to the tunnel I heard breaking glass.

Instinctively, I put out a hand to the edge of the opening and held my position.

Where had it come from? I couldn't tell. Being down in the water, below the top edge of the fake rocks that formed the cave, distorted the sounds.

More glass smashed, somebody yelled. Zimmer or Packard? Not Connie, I was sure.

And suddenly, overhead, colored lights came on.

If Zimmer was just about to bound up the steps, and then down to the loading dock, it was risky to stick my head up. But maybe he'd been diverted by the sounds and it might give me more options than trapping myself in a pitch-black cave.

I hesitated. I didn't hear running feet on the boards, nor any more shouting. Did I dare

creep back up to the top of the loading platform, above the dock, and sneak a look?

I did. I kept low and moved slowly, so as to
attract as little attention as possible. Maybe
Connie had managed to do something that
would lead Zimmer on a wild-goose chase long
enough for a miracle to happen. Like somebody calling the cops, and the cops actually
taking them seriously and showing up, sirens
screaming.

I reached the top of the platform, where the
walkway climbed over the rock wall before
going back down to the boats. And right at that
very moment, I heard the music.

A calliope, I thought, incredulous. Somebody had started the merry-go-round!

I saw Zimmer, then, only a few yards away
from me, but he was looking back over his
shoulder. I saw him yell, but couldn't make out
his words.

If I couldn't hear him from this close, Packard
wouldn't be able to, either.

As I crouched there, only my head above
the floor of the platform, lights began to come
on in the approaching dusk.

All over Wonderland, bright white lights and colored lights and neon signs advertising food and souvenirs and rides blinked on.

Not all at once, but a cluster at a time, spreading out from the area around the carousel the way ripples spread on the water when you drop in a stone.

No, not quite the same way. It was more like a wave going in one direction, sweeping over first one area, then the next.

Somebody was moving from one attraction to another, as fast as he could reach them, turning on lights and music. A window crashed as it broke, and moments later there was dance-hall music from the Wild West Village Saloon.

Connie and his keys, I thought, excitement almost suffocating me. Only he couldn't be doing it all alone. He couldn't reach both control buttons at the same time.

Julie? I thought suddenly. Could Julie be helping him? But we'd left Julie behind, outside in the RV park.

I saw Zimmer start to turn in my direction, and I jerked back. I wasn't fast enough. I bumped my chin on the top step and bit through my tongue so I tasted blood, and then I heard him running up the wooden steps toward me. I gave up trying to be careful.

I half fell down the steps and leaped into a gondola, and pushed off with my hands.

This time I didn't hesitate about entering the cave. Even a spooky dark pit was better than dealing with Zimmer, who didn't care if he broke both a guy's arms.

I only let the boat drift a little way on the circulating stream before I stopped it with a hand on the wall and listened.

Now Zimmer was closer, down inside the artificial rock mountain, standing on the loading dock.

"Come out, kid, and you won't get hurt," he said. I heard that quite clearly.

I didn't answer. Maybe I couldn't have, because it was hard enough just to breathe. Fat chance, I thought.

"If I have to come in after you," Zimmer said, "you'll be sorry."

I swallowed, steadying myself against the wall. The current wanted to carry my gondola along, and I searched for a bigger projection on the fake rock and held on harder.

Far in the distance, the calliope music came to an end. Only the whisper of the water beneath me broke the silence, except that the dance-hall music, a long way off, kept playing for another few minutes while I waited.

"You want to see your ma again, don't you?"

His voice sent shivers down my back.

"We got your ma and your little brother," Zimmer reminded me. He could speak more quietly now, and somehow that made his words more deadly. "Even without you, we're in control. You be nice and come out, and we'll take you to your mama. How's that?"

I jerked in alarm when I heard the other voice, sounding almost as nearby as Zimmer's. Packard had come to join him.

"I don't know what's going on, but I think we'd better pack up and get out of here. Those confounded kids have managed to turn everything on, and it covers all the sounds they make. The people in the trailer park will hear the music and investigate—or get the cops to do it—before long. Where's the other boy?"

"In here. Went in in a little boat. And now that you're here to make sure he doesn't escape, I'm going in after him," Zimmer said in a way that made my goose bumps bigger.

I eased up my grip on the wall and let the gondola float onward, keeping track of where I was by feel as I went around the corner. What if, I thought, when the wall receded and I knew I'd come to the first of the scenes set up to scare paying customers, I were to get out of my boat? Crawl up onto the ledge where the scene was laid out? If only I could think of a way to get the boat out of the way, so he wouldn't know I'd stopped, without having it come out the far end where Packard would see it and realize what I'd done.

There was no way to do that. The tunnel was only wide enough for one gondola at a time. When the one Zimmer was in got to me, it would bump into mine, whether I was in it or not.

Connie knew I'd gone for the cave, I thought. It was where he'd suggested I go, right from the start. Would he be able to think of anything to do to help me? Now that Packard was no longer guarding the hole through the fence, either Connie or Julie could slip back through it for help.

I'd started to slide away from the left-hand wall, and I leaned over, grabbing whatever I touched, throwing me off balance. I got a better hold and gave a small sigh of relief that I hadn't been pitched into the inky water.

The water. What about the water? How deep was it now? It wasn't the sluggish puddle we'd first found, not even up to Connie's knees, but a flowing stream that might be deep enough to conceal this flat-bottomed gondola if I could sink it.

It would have to be fast. Packard was giving Zimmer last-minute instructions, and he'd be showing up any minute.

Hoping I was guessing right about the depth of the water, and hanging on to an invisible figure on the ledge in front of me, I began to walk up the side of the gondola, forcing it to tip sideways.

The water, surprisingly cold, came over my foot, and then up my leg as I kept pushing the edge of the gondola downward. It only took seconds for it to fill with water; I scrambled up onto the ledge just before it sank.

I had been hanging on to a pirate's leg. I groped around, orienting myself in the darkness, and figured out where I was: with the pirate who held a lantern in the hook that replaced a missing hand, the one with a parrot on his shoulder.

I crawled around behind the pirate, crouched against the back of the ledge, and waited.

Chapter Seventeen

Zimmer didn't have any kind of light. Though I couldn't see him coming, I heard him. He wasn't making any effort to be quiet; in fact, he spoke to me as soon as he rounded the first turn in the tunnel and was in the dark, too.

"You better give up and come out, kid, if you know what's good for you."

I'd gotten pretty wet at the bottom of the Splasher, and it was always cooler inside the cave than outside because the sun never reached this far. So besides having goose bumps because I was scared, I was actually cold.

My teeth were starting to chatter, and I bit them together so Zimmer wouldn't hear me.

When he spoke right alongside me the hair lifted off my scalp.

For a minute I thought he'd seen me when

he said, "Come on now, don't be an idiot. If you don't give up, we're going to have to be mean to your little brother. You hear him screaming, it'll be too late to save him."

There was the sound of his gondola bumping the wall right in front of me, and I froze. What if the water wasn't deep enough? What if his boat hung up on the one I'd sunk?

And then he was past, and he was still talking to me, making threats. He hadn't seen me, and his gondola had gone right over the top of the first one.

I just waited, shivering.

I could faintly hear the carousel again, the calliope music. And maybe—was it my imagination?—voices shouting. I waited until I wanted to scream; surely Zimmer had had time to go all the way out the other end.

Finally I couldn't stand it any longer. I edged forward and slid off my ledge into the water, praying it wasn't so deep I'd have to swim. I had a nightmare once about swimming in black water, in the dark.

It was cold, and it came to a little above my waist. I stepped onto the sunken gondola, nearly tripped getting out of it, and headed toward the entrance, hoping they wouldn't be expecting me to go back the way I'd come.

Dusk had deepened, though it wasn't really dark yet, and there were lights on all over inside the park. I sucked in a breath when I realized Packard was standing on the platform above the loading dock, and he was holding Kenny by the back of the shirt.

Though I couldn't see Kenny's face, he seemed to be all right. For now, but for how long?

I guess Packard thought too much time had passed, too. He was looking toward the opposite opening, and he yelled. "Zimmer! What are you doing? Haven't you found him yet?"

"He ain't in here," Zimmer called back, and a moment later his gondola drifted out into the open. "I went all the way through, and the kid's not there."

"That's crazy, he's got to be in there! He took one of those boats and he went in the other end, didn't he? You must have missed him."

"How could I miss him?" Zimmer was in a

worse humor than before, and he didn't like Packard yelling at him. As soon as I saw him, I'd jerked back inside the opening, but stayed close enough so I could hear. "It's just a tunnel that winds around and comes back out; there's no place else to go."

"Well, go through again. You must have missed him somehow," Packard insisted. "Check the walls on both sides, make sure there isn't a side tunnel or something."

"You go through," Zimmer said sullenly. "This isn't turning out the way you said. A quarter of the value of that load ain't enough to make it worth my while to go chasing around in a dark hole looking for a bratty kid. Let's take the other one back to Sophie and go to work on 'em."

I was frozen, inside and out. What should I do now? I wondered desperately.

Packard called his partner a name, and then he said, "All right, you watch this one. I'll go find the other one myself. He *has* to be in there somewhere."

I heard them moving around on the dock, and I started backing away, then turned and made my way deep inside again, afraid and not knowing what else to do.

I hadn't thought about the fact that I'd climbed onto the first of the rocky shelves from the edge of the sunken gondola, not from the floor of the artificial stream. It was too high up, and I panicked for a minute until I located the sunken boat again. Even then, it was hard work dragging myself out of the water, and I was afraid Packard would get there before I did.

Packard talked to me, too, in a deadly voice that convinced me he wouldn't hesitate to hurt me—and Kenny and Ma too—if he didn't get what he wanted.

He was coming alongside me, now, and I shivered against the back wall of the ledge, wondering if he'd go on past, too, or if he'd notice that the ledge was there. Once he realized there were a series of ledges, he'd investigate and find me for sure.

What did I do then?

He was talking, and he stopped in the middle of a sentence. He'd realized the upper wall had changed. I forgot to breathe.

And then, expecting to feel his hand on my ankle any minute, I was suddenly blinded when the light came on.

It wasn't a bright light, but the one intended to make this scene look spooky, and it was more of a surprise to Packard than it was to me.

I don't know where I got the nerve to throw all my weight behind the pirate and shove him forward, with the hooked hand and its lantern plunging right into Packard's face.

A second later the lights went out and it was dark again. I knew where I was, and I stayed there, but Packard was cursing and thrashing around. From the sounds he made, I guessed he'd fallen into the bottom of the boat, maybe cracking his head.

By the time he'd recovered, the gondola had drifted past me. Zimmer started yelling from outside.

"What's going on? Packard? What happened?"

The tunnel curved, so when the lights came on at the next scene I could barely tell it except that Packard started swearing again. I don't suppose he was scared, once he realized what was happening, but he'd been startled enough the first time to allow himself to be swept on past me.

Although the tunnel was fairly long, it curved back on itself in a tight pattern; it was easy to hear what was happening beyond the spot where I was because the walls weren't real rock and nothing was very far away.

When the crazy laughter began, it echoed through the cavern. After it finally died away, Zimmer demanded, "What's going on? What was that?" He sounded quite unnerved.

"It's a fool tourist-trap fun house," Packard yelled, startlingly near. "I'll be out in a minute. This can't last much longer."

"You find the kid?"

"Not yet. But I will."

I was stunned. Hadn't he seen me when the light exposed the pirate I'd shoved at him? Maybe not. He'd been taken off guard, and the light had only been on for a matter of seconds. Had he gotten such a poor look at me that he'd taken me for part of the pirate scene?

The laughter, though, wasn't part of the

stuff programmed to scare the customers. Connie was here somewhere. I'd know that fake laugh anywhere. It had sure scared *me* the first time I heard it.

I didn't know whether to stay on my ledge or get back in the water and return to the mouth of the cave. Once Packard was outside, if they didn't yell, I might not know what they were saying, and I decided I needed to hear them. So I slid into the water again. I was already wet, and this time it didn't feel quite so cold.

I got to the entrance about the same time Packard came out the exit ten yards away.

"There has to be another way out of here," he declared angrily as his gondola bumped the dock. "The kid got away somehow."

I held my breath. Would they leave if they thought that?

Without warning, every light in the park went out and all the music stopped.

I knew it had to be Connie or Julie who'd thrown the switch, but what for? Grown men wouldn't be scared of the dark, would they? They might be confused, but it wasn't really dark enough to frighten an adult.

The voice that came over a loudspeaker was familiar, but it had a ring of authority that was new.

"This is the police. You are surrounded. Surrender your hostages and come out with your hands up. Walk to the center of the park, near the carousel. I repeat, with your hands up. You have three minutes. I repeat, you are surrounded by armed police officers."

For a moment there was no reaction from the two men. Then Zimmer shoved Kenny to one side and started up the steps from the dock. "I'm getting out of here. I don't know what's going on, but I don't care anymore. I'm leaving."

"That's not the cops," Packard snarled. "It's those kids, they've got hold of a microphone somewhere!"

"I don't care who it is. I've had it," Zimmer said, and then he was gone.

Packard hadn't given up yet. I heard Kenny give a protesting cry when Packard grabbed his arm and dragged him away from the entrance to the Pirate's Cave. By then no one was paying any attention to where I was.

Packard didn't even look back when I followed him up and out onto the grounds.

The man was walking fast, dragging Kenny, but he wasn't running. I couldn't let him take Kenny, I thought, and I *did* run, though I was afraid he'd hear me, even on the grass.

Packard was sticking to the path, heading toward the place he'd come into the park after us. I didn't watch where I was going, and I tripped over one of the good-sized rocks that outlined the pathway.

I don't even remember thinking about it. I bent, picked up one of the stones, about the size of the one I'd thrown through the window of the castle-office, and hurled it.

Pa and I used to play catch in the park, and he said I had a pretty good arm for a skinny kid. I put everything I had behind it.

The rock hit Packard in the back.

I heard the air go out of him, and he let go of Kenny and started to turn around.

"Run, Kenny!" I yelled, but it was already too late. Packard had already grabbed him again.

I found another rock, but my aim wasn't

quite as good this time—it was different with the man facing me, and so close—but it clipped his cheek and he jerked.

And then the lights came on again, though there was no music, and this time the voice that spoke didn't sound like Connie's version of the The Insane Dr. Murder.

"This is the police. Put your hands up and stand where you are."

For a minute I thought he was going to obey. Kenny pulled against him, and then Packard made up his mind. He jerked Kenny right off his feet, so Kenny yelped before he got scooped up and half carried, half dragged along with Packard.

I just stood there, watching them disappear beyond the Wild West Village Saloon, feeling helpless.

The police were really there, though. That wasn't Connie repeating orders over a bullhorn, it was real cops. I ran toward the hole in the fence, hoping that Packard wouldn't find the way out through the drainpipe. The cops would catch him and make him give up Kenny, wouldn't they?

Connie said later he was real disappointed that the cops didn't use sirens, but of course they were coming because of what Uncle Henry had told them, not because they knew what was happening to us.

The movable boards had been torn out of the fence by the time I got there, making more room for bigger people to go through, and there was a crowd on the other side.

The purple bus was back, not in Uncle Henry's space but parked in the middle of the road behind the black sedan so it was pinned in. Everybody who lived in Wonderland RV Park was there, including Mrs. Giuliani's dog, who wouldn't stop barking.

"I saw that man banging the boy against the fence," Mrs. Giuliani was telling someone, probably for the tenth time, "and I called the police."

It turned out practically everybody had called them. Uncle Henry had convinced them we had some genuine evidence that Ma had been kidnapped. Mrs. Biggers called them when the men returned after she'd told them she wouldn't allow them to take Kenny and me, no matter what their note said. Mr. Alvinhorst had used the pay phone to call when he heard music and then saw lights inside of Wonderland.

I practically fell out into the midst of all those people. Uncle Henry pushed through them to reach me, and I gasped out that Packard still had Kenny.

There was only one police car, and the officer had already put handcuffs on Zimmer, who glowered at me through the back window.

Uncle Henry called to the officer. "The other one still has the younger boy!"

"We've got more officers on the way," the cop said, and right then we heard them coming. Code three, with sirens. "Is there another way out of the amusement park, son?"

Connie and I both told him at once about the drainpipe. "It would be a tight squeeze for a grown man, though," Connie added.

Three more cars filled up the driveway behind the first patrol car, and more police officers jumped out. They all had a consultation, and in just a few seconds they were spreading out to surround Wonderland. I heard one of them say, "He's got a hostage," and I felt sickish. His hostage was Kenny.

A pair of plainclothes officers arrived right behind the patrol cars and started asking questions. One of them sat in the car with Zimmer and talked through that mesh between the seats. The other one talked to Connie and Julie and me. Uncle Henry stood with his hand on my shoulder, and he sounded angry when he finally spoke.

"We've been trying for several days to make somebody believe Sophie had been kidnapped. From what the boys say, it sounds like Sophie found out something—"

"They mentioned a tape," I put in, "that Ma swiped before it could be erased. We didn't find anything like that."

The officer, who had introduced himself as Sergeant Patterson, considered that, then stepped over to the car where his partner was talking to a sullen-looking Zimmer.

That officer nodded at the sergeant. "I think this one's going to be cooperative. I read him his rights, and he's asked for a lawyer, but he's already admitted they kidnapped Mrs. Van Huler."

"Where is she?" I demanded. "Where's my ma? Is she all right?"

Zimmer just scowled at me, but he'd been talking, all right.

"They left her locked up in a warehouse. A patrol car has been dispatched out there; we'll be hearing from them shortly."

"What's this about a tape that's missing?" Sergeant Patterson asked.

Zimmer scowled at him too. "I'm waiting for my lawyer," he said.

"Fine. He'll meet you down at the jail, after we've booked you," the officer said stolidly. "I can make an educated guess, though. Lot of those trucking places record their incoming phone calls, when people make arrangements to have things shipped. Just to keep it all straight until the dispatcher can get it written down on a board."

I remembered then. "Yeah! They have a big white board behind the desk, with every driver's name written on it, and where they're going. Sometimes Ma helps write that stuff in, if Cranston's busy. I saw her, once."

The cop nodded. "That it, Zimmer? Something

on the tape made Mrs. Van Huler suspicious?"

Zimmer just grunted and didn't answer.

Actually, we didn't have to wait too long to find out about that. We could hear the cops talking on the bullhorns inside Wonderland, and it was pretty clear they hadn't found Packard and Kenny yet.

They did find Ma, though. When his radio squawked, Sergeant Patterson went back to his car to answer it and came back to let us know. "Your mom's okay. She's worried about you kids, and they're going to bring her over here. They're only a few miles away; it won't take them long."

I hoped real hard that they'd have Kenny back, and safe, before Ma got there, but they didn't.

When Ma got out of the police car and ran toward us, I hugged her, and she almost broke my ribs hugging back. "Where's Kenny?" she asked.

Ma was tired and dirty and there was a dark bruise on her cheek. She looked anxiously past me at the sergeant. "You haven't got Kenny yet?"

"The man named Packard is holding him hostage," I told her, and it was all I could do not to cry.

Sergeant Patterson spoke quietly while another officer started trying to get all the people to move back away from the hole in the fence. "We'll get your son back, Mrs. Van Huler. Packard is trapped in there; he can't get away, and he has nothing to gain by hurting the boy now. Why don't you and Rick go sit in my car while we take care of this?"

"I guess I do need to sit down again," Ma said, putting an arm around me.

Julie and Connie came with us, too, when I asked them. So we sat in the unmarked car—I could tell by Connie's eyes as he looked it over that he was planning what he'd say to his friends about all this—and Ma told us what had been happening to her.

I heard everything she said, but the whole time I kept watching the opening in the fence, crossing my fingers that Kenny would come safely through it.

Chapter Eighteen

We sat in Sergeant Patterson's car, and Ma was so nervous about Kenny and Packard that she had a hard time telling us what had been happening. I guess she wouldn't have said anything if we hadn't kept asking questions.

"He's a terrible man," she said, shivering. "He pretends to be friendly and pleasant, but he doesn't care who he cheats . . . or hurts."

I looked at the bruise on her cheek. "Did he do that?" I asked, sounding croaky.

Ma glanced into the rearview mirror and touched the discolored place. "Zimmer shoved me into that storage room where they put me after I got away and tried to call you. I fell and hit something hard."

Connie had just met her, but he wasn't

bashful. "How come you didn't just call the cops instead of trying to call Mr. Svoboda?"

Ma never took her eyes off the police officer standing at the corner of the laundry building, where he could watch the hole in the fence. "I should have, I guess. But I had to know if the boys were safe; Zimmer said they were going to hurt Rick and Kenny. . . ." Tears welled up in her eyes. "I was afraid if I called the police and he had the kids—"

She broke off, and we all knew what she'd been afraid of. And we were still afraid for Kenny, even though we didn't see how Packard could get him out of the amusement park with all the cops around.

"And then they came after you, in the phone booth," I prompted, "before you could call the cops. And locked you up in a different place. We almost found you, Ma, at that wrecking yard."

She reached over and squeezed my hand, giving me a watery smile. I decided not to ask what Zimmer and Packard had threatened to do to Kenny and me. Maybe I'd be better off not knowing for sure.

"So what's it all about?" Connie wanted to know. And, still watching the police officers in case anything developed about rescuing Kenny, Ma started to explain.

She was sorry she'd doubted Pa's innocence in the hijacking even for a minute. She worried they might fire him, and she kept trying to figure things out.

About a week after Pa left, she read in the paper about another hijacking, a load belonging to Ajax Tires being hauled by Costa Trucking, which was only a few blocks from E & F. It sounded a lot like what had happened to Pa.

The week after that, she heard that Baylord Electronics, who often shipped with E & F, had lost a load of very expensive computer components, while they were being hauled to California by JV Trucking.

It seemed kind of a coincidence at first, because J V Trucking was right across the road from E & F. The secretaries and bookkeepers for all three trucking companies often had lunch together at Josie's Place, a little café that was the only eating place within walking distance of where they worked.

The next time they got together, they talked about the hijackings, and how upsetting it was both to the truckers who did the hauling and to the owners of the cargo. And Ma learned that all three trucking firms were insured by the same insurance company, the one Packard worked for as an adjuster.

At first she didn't think so much of that, but she kept worrying about Pa and what would happen to him if he had another load stolen. He could lose his job, and if anybody thought he had anything to do with the hijackings he might not be able to find another one.

Then while she was doing her bookkeeping she noticed the names of all the companies that had lost loads and got to thinking about the fact that every time a hijacking had happened the trucks had been loaded with the most valuable stuff. And Ma wondered how the hijackers had known just which loads would be the easiest ones to sell to unscrupulous buyers for the biggest profits.

On impulse she copied the pages out of her ledgers with the lists of shippers' names to take home and study and think about. She didn't want to go to either Mr. Edward or Mr. Frank, because right then she even suspected they might be defrauding their own insurance company. She didn't trust anybody. But she decided to do some research and see if she could figure out any kind of pattern to the hijackings.

She stuck the copies with her purse to take home, thinking that maybe she'd talk to the secretaries and bookkeepers at the other companies and see if there had been hijackings she hadn't heard about. She was trying to think who could possibly know, from at least three different trucking companies, about those valuable loads and where it would be feasible to hijack them.

And then, because the office was busy and the dispatcher, Cranston, was having some kind of meeting with Mr. Edward and Mr. Frank in one of their offices, Ma did something she almost never did.

She answered the phone that usually only Cranston answered, took an order to haul a load of fertilizer to Illinois, and noticed when she'd finished that there wasn't much space left on the tape that recorded such calls.

"I decided to do Cranston a favor," she told us, "and check the tape to make sure everything that had been recorded was written up on the board, including the one I'd just contracted for. I didn't know which driver Cranston would give that load to, but he could fill that part in later, and I put a new tape on the machine for the next calls."

Ordinarily, Cranston would have been the only one who'd ever have heard any of those tapes. But when Ma rewound the tape and started listening to it on the little tape player the dispatcher kept for that purpose, practically the first thing she heard was a conversation that made her suspect that Cranston was involved in an inside job.

"He took the order from an electronics company, and I knew that load would be worth hundreds of thousands of dollars. There wasn't anything suspicious about that, we haul that kind of stuff all the time," she told us, never taking her eyes off the cop watching the fence, in case Kenny came through it. "But right after that call, Cranston made one of his own. Didn't call anybody by name, didn't identify himself. He just said 'Tri Cities Electronics. I'll give it to Baker; he always stops at Monte's Truck Stop. He should be there tomorrow night, about nine.'" That was all, but I felt like somebody'd kicked me in the stomach. There was no reason, no *legitimate* reason, why Cranston should have passed that information on to anyone else. And though the man he'd called had only spoken a few words when he picked up the phone, I had a feeling the voice was one I'd heard, only I couldn't remember who it was."

Ma squeezed my hand hard, as if it made her feel better to hang on to somebody, and kept on talking.

"I rewound the tape to the beginning, thinking maybe I'd better pretend I hadn't listened to it, but before I was quite finished getting it off the machine, Cranston came back."

He hadn't paid any attention to her, but Ma was afraid to take the tape out of the tape player for fear he'd see it and realize she'd listened to it.

"At first I thought I'd put it in the basket where he keeps the used tapes until he reuses them," Ma said, "but in the meantime I didn't dare touch it. And then he went outside to the shop for a few minutes, and I decided to stick the tape in my purse and take it home and listen to the whole thing. I was positive by then that Cranston was telling somebody about the loads to hijack, and I didn't know if there was anybody I could trust; but I was going to ask your pa about it when he came in from that trip."

Connie'd kept still for a long time. Now he leaned over the back of the front seat. "Only they figured out you were onto them."

"Yes. Cranston realized the tape on the phone had been changed, and that I was the only one who could have done it. If I'd dropped it in the basket the way I should have, he'd probably have thought I hadn't listened to it. Anyway, I got on the bus and went home, and I thought I'd gotten away with it until those thugs caught up with me."

"Zimmer and Packard," Julie said. "They're scary."

"They sure are," Ma agreed. "When I got off the bus near home and they drove up alongside of me, they scared me half to death. I didn't know Zimmer, but Packard is in and out of the office all the time with various kinds of business. The minute he spoke to me, I knew he was the one Cranston had called with that information about a shipment. When I saw the boys coming, all I could think of was to get them away from me, because I didn't want them mixed up in whatever Packard intended to do."

Connie couldn't wait for her to tell it herself. He leaned forward. "So you stuck the papers in Rick's notebook, then dropped it on the steps so they wouldn't get it."

"I dropped it accidentally," Ma said. "The papers weren't particularly incriminating, though they did have a list of customers that included the ones who'd lost loads when they were hijacked and the one I suspected they *intended* to steal from next. Packard said they wanted to talk to me, and kept trying to get me into the car. I pretended I didn't know what they were talking about, insisted I had to get home right away, and practically ran. I knew if they found that tape on me they'd do something to stop me from ever telling anybody about it—"

"So where is it?" I interrupted. "Did they get it back?"

Ma shook her head. "No. I ran up the steps and into our apartment house, but they came after me before the door latched behind me and followed upstairs. I only had a few seconds before they got there. I was so frantic I didn't even get that door locked, either. All I could think of was getting rid of that incriminating tape."

"So where is it?" I demanded. "They came back and searched for it. They made an awful mess."

Ma almost grinned a little. "There was a sweatshirt of yours on the floor beside the table just inside the front door. Right where you dropped it, instead of hanging it up. I stuck the tape in one pocket, just seconds before they got there."

"And I packed it with my other clothes when we went with Uncle Henry," I said. "Only it never got cold enough to wear it, so I didn't find the tape."

"And you didn't tell them where it was, so they kidnapped you," Julie said to Ma, looking horrified. "And they hurt you."

"Not as much as I was afraid they were going to," Ma said. "They decided it would be easier to take Rick and Kenny hostage. They knew I'd have to do what they said if they had my boys, and I didn't know how I was going to get out of it."

"But even if you cooperated then," Connie said soberly, "they might not have let you all go."

He meant, I thought, gulping, that they might have killed all of us to keep us quiet.

Ma nodded, and her face was grim. "They said they'd just leave us all locked up, and when they got to Mexico they'd call somebody and tell them where to find us before we starved."

And if anybody believed that, I thought, they probably believed in fairies and the pot of gold at the end of the rainbow. It made me feel sick, and I prayed that the cops would get Kenny away from Packard real quick.

Right then we heard the shot.

Ma turned pale and jumped out of the car.

The rest of us were right behind her, but the cop was waving everybody back from the laundry building.

A minute later, when Ma was hanging on to me so hard it hurt, Mrs. Giuliani's dog began to bark wildly and jerked his leash free of her hand. He ran right through the laundry and Mrs. Giuliani tore after him, and then all of a sudden people pushed forward and started cheering.

Because the police were coming through the building from the hole in the fence behind it, and they had Packard and Kenny.

Kenny was beaming as we ran toward him, and Ma almost squashed him in a big hug.

"I bit him," Kenny said proudly. "That nasty man tried to take me up where he could drop me off the rolly coaster if they didn't let him go, so I bit him. He let go of me, and I ran. He tried to catch me, but a cop shot him, and I got away."

Packard wasn't hurt very bad, I guessed. He was walking with a cop hanging on to him on each side, but there was blood on his shoulder. He didn't look at anybody when they put him into one of the patrol cars.

It was all over, except for everybody having to tell the police everything.

Connie and Julie told how they'd found the keys, activated the rides and the music and the lights, and how Connie even realized when he found the microphone setup that it could be made to broadcast over the entire park. He'd sneaked up close enough to set the operation going in the Pirate Cave, so that the lights were triggered by moving gondolas as they were supposed to be, and then broadcast his well-practiced laughter. I told Connie if the park had still been open, they'd have recorded it to play every time they had a customer go through the cave.

They were the heroes, but the next day they put my picture in the paper, too, and they said I'd cleverly outwitted the crooks by hiding in the Pirate Cave.

Right then, though, it was mostly just a relief to know that Packard and Zimmer weren't going to get a chance to torture us to keep Ma quiet until they'd hijacked one more quarter-million-dollar load. They'd caught up with Pa and told him they had his wife and kids and that if he didn't cooperate, too, they'd shoot all of us. Once they disposed of that last load, they were all going to take the money and run for South America where the U.S. authorities couldn't get at them.

It told all about it in the paper. How Ma had found out about their scheme to steal valuable loads from several different trucking companies. There were more than the ones Ma knew about.

Packard had been setting up hijackings for quite a while. He had persuaded dispatchers from several firms to tip him off to when something valuable and easily fenced would be shipped, like Pa's load of television sets, in return for a share of the profits. Because Packard was an insurance adjuster for a lot of trucking companies, he had a legitimate excuse to be talking to dispatchers or any other employees.

Once they knew where a truckload of something they wanted was going to be, they simply had somebody approach the driver and divert his attention one way or another, like offering Pa a steak dinner and eating with him to make sure he didn't leave the restaurant until the thief had time to hijack the load.

They didn't care if suspicion fell on the driver of the stolen trailer, or if he lost his job. All they cared about was the money they made.

If Ma hadn't worked in the same office as the dispatcher, Bob Cranston, and if she hadn't been trying to figure out whether or not Pa was involved in the hijacking, they might have gone on doing it forever.

I felt kind of limp after they'd finally taken Zimmer and Packard away. All the people who lived in the RV park were standing around talking, unwilling to go back to their TV after the live action in their backyard.

I was glad when Uncle Henry suggested Ma go into the purple bus and clean up, and then we'd have something to eat. Everybody was suddenly starving, especially Ma.

"I'd like that," Ma said. "They didn't bother to feed me much the whole time they had me locked up."

"Ma," Kenny said, tugging at her arm, "can we go back into Wonderland now that the lights are on and everything will run? Can I ride the merry-go-round?"

Everybody looked at him. Ma made a sort of tired little gurgling sound of laughter. "Oh, honey," she said, "let's just go home where I can have a bath and something to eat besides greasy hamburgers!"

"Hot dogs?" Kenny asked, brightening. "And then we could come back. Doesn't anybody else want to ride the merry-go-round?"

"Sure," Julie said, and Connie nodded.

"If they're going to tear it all down, we ought to ride on everything once more," Connie said.

"Not tonight," Uncle Henry said firmly. "Maybe tomorrow, if they'll let us."

And they did. The next day we came back and everybody from the RV park got a chance to ride the merry-go-round, though some of them just stood and watched and listened to the music. We got permission from the granddaughter of Mr. Mixon who had wanted to keep the park open. Reporters even came and took our pictures, and the story was on the front page of the paper.

When people read about it, there were a lot of calls to Mrs. Biggers, offering places for the people who lived there to move their trailers.

I hoped when Pa came home he and Ma would get back together again. It hasn't happened yet, though he did come to see us and hugged everybody, even Ma.

But we got away from Packard and Zimmer. We got Ma back. So maybe good things will happen in threes, too.

Anyway, I'm still hoping.